MAXINE

JACK REMICK

A Quartet Global Book

MAXINE

JACK REMICK

This is a work of fiction.
All the characters in this novella
are creatures of my own making
Author permission required to use any text
Cover image © 2020 by Meredith Bricken Mills
Maxine © 2020 by Jack Remick
A Quartet Global Book

ISBN: 978-0-9914258-5-3

MAXINE

Every story is a love story.
Every story is a detective story.

In the Beginning There Was Reno

She is parked on a stool at an empty blackjack table, all legs and nylons and blue tight sweater, no bra—bait on the hook. She reads me up and down and I see the sex in her eyes, in that slow lowering of the lids. I say,

Can I buy you a drink?

When she picks up her chips I see the diamond on her finger—it's like that, my radar only works for women with that band on a hand that says Taboo, Bud. I push it away, don't like it. Some people go to Reno to gamble, I go to Reno to hunt. I'm not sure what I'm hunting for—maybe the other half of my soul, something to make me whole, something to fill in the gaps and plaster over the chinks in my psyche. She slides off the stool and I follow her to the elevator. She has black hair down to her shoulders and it glistens in the neon lights like a jackpot spewing from a one-armed bandit. She pushes the elevator button for floor fourteen with her diamond-studded hand and leans against the wall of the elevator and looks at me like a doctor diagnosing my disease. My disease—it's genetic, I suppose, something in my blood that won't let me connect to a woman unless she's got I'm Married tattooed across her forehead.

She leads me out of the elevator to her room—the hallway cool and crisp—it's always cool in the dens of iniquity. She holds up at the door, card key in hand, that moment of regret at the threshold when she is asking herself the question. Is this the one who will kill me? I touch her waist. She quivers. Turning, she looks up at me and says,

No chains or whips, all right?

*****

I lie on the bed and watch her wrap up in a pale pink hotel terry cloth robe. Her black hair hangs sweaty hot and stringy like a horse after two furlongs. Her eyes, still glazed, her gorge still flushed she leans down giving me a front row view of the rose tattooed on the swell of her breast. She whispers,

Don't go anywhere.

Wheeling, she dances to the door and holds it open and the smiling waiter from room service enters pushing a cart loaded with breakfast. He says,

Will there be anything else?

You can take the trays from last night, she says.

Sorry ma'am, he says, the Do Not Disturb sign was on the door.

He loads the dinner plates and the silver covers and the forks and knives and the claws of two crabs and the bones still slick with butter. Pushing the cart like a gravedigger, he bows out. She turns to me and opens the robe and she says,

You want dessert first?

Gotta refuel, I say.

You're no fun.

She wraps the robe tight at the waist and pushes the breakfast cart to the bed and sits down, cross legged. The robe falls open over her tanned legs and I see the string of blue leaves tattooed on the inside of her left thigh. I say,

Why did you do that?

Do what?

Cover up when he came. It's Reno. Nakedness is half the fun.

She plucks a piece of toast from the warmer, spoons a dollop of strawberry jam on it, takes a delicate bite. Chewing, she says,

I'm not an exhibitionist.

I touch the blue leaves. Run my finger over the tattoo and up into the crease of her thigh and leave it there and she shudders and closes her eyes and drops the toast on the tray. I kiss her belly and up to her breasts and the rose tattoo and then her lips. She says,

Can I take that hand with me when I go home?

I like your tats.

She smiles. Pulling free, she sits on her knees on the bed and pours two cups of coffee. Then, like an old married couple we eat in silence—eggs benedict, bacon, toast, yogurt, coffee. When she pours the second cup, she lays a hand on my arm. The long slender fingers with her ruby red nails glisten. The big gaudy perfect diamond in its platinum setting rose like a blister on her hand. She says,

You know I like you.

I like you too or I wouldn't be here.

I'd like you better if I knew your name.

Let me guess your real name isn't Yosanda, right?

I could have looked in your wallet while you were in the shower.

Why didn't you?

I was tempted.

But you didn't.

No. I didn't want to violate your...your trust.

Why don't you take off the rock?

She pulls her hand back, brushes the diamond against the terry cloth robe. She says,

It didn't stop you, did it?

I'm sick. I'm addicted to married women.

Because we're safe? Because it can't get serious? Because it doesn't follow you home?

All of that.

You get what you need, she says, why can't you give me what I need?

What is that?

Tell me your name.

What's so magic about a name?

I just like to know.

You mean you need to know.

You can be so cruel, she says.

She gets on her hands and knees to crawl off the bed. I watch her behind. The pink robe stretches tight across her butt and I reach for her and she stops and looks back at me as my hand slides under the robe and she shimmies and closes her almond eyes and I draw my hand back, moist. Her hair still damp clings in clumps to her neck. I roll her over, open the robe and she opens up, the robe falling away. She raises her knees. She pulls me into that rose on her breast and I taste her nipple, kiss the sweet valley between her breasts. Her heat against my skin. I enter her and she shudders the way she shuddered the first time and she rakes her nails, those long, ruby red nails across my back and the fire—eight lanes wide—burns into me. She whispers,

This is what you need, isn't it?

You get what you want, I get what I need.

He never does that to me. It's illegal, isn't it? What you're doing to me?

You talk too much.

Coming loosens my tongue, she says.

Okay. It's illegal only if you get caught.

Do you want to get caught?

Does he have a PI tracking you?

He doesn't want to know. It would be expensive to find out.

Is that why you do this? To hurt him?

And when we finish, she lays on her belly, head on the soft white pillow where a few crumbs of toast mar the satin coverlet. I roll onto my side. That's the way it was going to be—breakfast, sex, sleep, ask me my name.

Well, she says, does a fuck like that earn me the right to know your name?

It was the first time she's said anything Anglo-Saxon. The words don't fit in her mouth. They don't come out of her mouth pretty. Everything else about the mouth is pretty, almost pristine in its eagerness. It is the kind of mouth a man could love for a long time because of the things it did. I tap her lips with my index finger to shut her up. She says,

That's what it is, isn't it? Two strangers fucking.

You don't need to talk like that.

Now you're mad at me. She says. You get what you need before you treat me like dirt.

Did you get the name of the bald-headed guy? I say.

She rolls over and sits up, glistening. Her sweat-streaked hair, more glorious than before, falling over the rose tattoo on her breast. She says,

How did you know about that?

I watched the way you handled him.

You a god damned private eye?

Do I look like a private eye?

You were spying on me.

He didn't have what you wanted?

He wasn't ashamed to tell me his name, she says. His name was Bill Alexander and he said he wasn't married but he was wearing a ring. He said he's from San Francisco. Poor Bill, he lasted only five minutes.

Why did you let him off the hook?

He wanted to pay me so I threw him out.

Lucky me. Three days and I'm still here.

Does that tell you something?

It tells me we've spent three days—getting everything we want.

Almost everything, she says.

She looks at her diamond, spreads her fingers. I say,

Do you have them all sign your yearbook?

I don't keep a book.

So my name doesn't really matter, I say.

Please. You can trust me. You know you can trust me.

There is something plaintive in her voice then, a kind of suppressed wail that hangs up in her throat and squeaks out and I feel sorry for her and bad for her and I ease up on the hook before jerking it tight again just to watch her squirm.

Okay, I say. Guy, my name is Guy.

What did your mother call you?

Anonymous, I say. Anonymous Guy.

So the honeymoon is over, Anonymous Guy.

It's the way it has to be.

That's what you need, isn't it? She says. The cheating part. It only works for you if there's betrayal in the equation, right?

What works for you? Yosanda.

I slide my palm over her leg, brushing at the cluster of blue leaves inked into her skin. I lean down and kiss the tattoo. I see then that the cluster is a bouquet and the ink is in different shades of blue and then it comes to me that this is how she keeps track...every year she adds a new leaf to the daisy chain on her thigh. Every year she cuts a memory into her skin and next year some new guy will run his fingers over my leaf and she'll keep doing it until the chain of leaves runs all the way around her thigh and then what? My fingers nestle between her legs where she is still wet and slick and again she arches her back and she comes and this time she is soaking and she sobs if she is in pain and the scent of her sex wafts over me and she collapses and a guttural rasp—an animal with its throat cut—escapes her lips.

*****

In the light washing out of the bathroom I see the glint of the diamond on her and smell the sweetness still of her sweat on my hands. She isn't afraid of anything, wants to try it all, doesn't want to die wondering. I've never been there before—that close to feeling complete and wanted. It's almost enough to fill the void.

I watch her twist her hair up in a do that says I'm getting ready to fly back to Fresno, back to my no good limp dick husband who doesn't care if I go to Reno and gamble away a hundred thousand dollars and get laid for three nights and two days—that kind of hair do. Watching her, I remember tangling my fingers in that nest, holding her face down on the bed, hard in her until she begged me to let her come. And then rolling over, thanking me for it, asking for more.

She stands in the doorway to the bathroom, her sins bound up in virgin white cotton. She says,

Why are you being so mysterious?

You know all my secrets, I say. Look at me.

I pull the sheet off and she laughs and whirls around and I watch her white pantied butt, all thirty-five years of it, sashay away. I lean into the baroque, rococo headboard with its carved angels and demons—pitch forks and harps listing in eternal battle and I wonder how many times Oh God, Oh God has bounced off those cherubim on that bed in this room in this hotel in this city. You multiply by ten million and you get the dead sperm-count, the scratched backs, the bitten lips and a thousand other crimes.

She emerges, dolled up—the short skirt gone, the black Brazilian gone, the tight blue sweater packed in its bag. She wears a white linen pant suit, black stockings, a plain gray blouse buttoned to the neck. She's different, this one. I'm a hit and run kind of guy, catch and release, get the job done and then move on, but there's something in the way she walks that tells me maybe she's for real. She says,

How do I look, Anonymous Guy?

Come here, I say.

Nah uh, she says.

But she sits on the edge of the bed and she runs that hand with that diamond up my thigh and she says,

I hate to leave while there's still work to be done but I gotta get back. He gives me just a week a year to work it out of my system.

Ritual, I say. Cleanses the soul.

I sit up, pull away from her. She says,

What are you covering up, Anonymous Guy?

What makes you think I'm covering something up?

In that elevator you were a complete mystery, but now I just feel your agony.

You have a lot of practice at reading secrets?

You know a lot about me, she says, and I know next to nothing about you.

That's good.

Good? I don't want good. I come to Sin City to let out the bad.

And you're very good at it. Anything left? A tip for the bellboy maybe? I hear they like leftovers.

You don't have to be crude.

Crude worked when I had you on your knees.

You're just trying to hurt me now.

She lets go of my cock. Stands up. Smooths the linen suit over her hips, getting the wrinkles out, thinking everything will be all right if she gets the wrinkles out, but they don't come out, they never come out. She raises her hand with her diamond on it and the stone glitters in the light and she strokes her hair now untangled, unknotted, no longer sweat-soaked. She says,

Will I see you again?

Probably not.

What if I want to see you again?

I get here every six months or so.

I'll pencil it in, she says.

I watch her mouth. It's a sweet mouth, a sad mouth that didn't mind going the distance, didn't mind taking everything in, letting nothing out until there was nothing left to come out. Smooth lips. Just before she got out of bed, she kissed me. No tongue. Just lips. The kind of chaste good-bye kiss you lay on your boy friend the night you break up with him. He knows you never want to see him again. There was a tear in her eye. One glistening tear drop. She says,

You're a strange one.

Not strange, just messed up beyond repair.

Oh Christ, she mumbles. I don't know what's gotten into me. I don't even know where you're from.

You don't need to know.

This never happened before. I don't want to go back to him. I can't go back there. Are you going to say something?

You had me confused at first, I say. I thought you were a hooker, but then I saw the diamond.

I hate you, she says. You don't have a feeling in that glorious body, do you?

Taking a deep breath she stands straight, tucks at the gray blouse already perfect in the waistband of her linen suit. Getting it under control again, she dabs at her eyes where an honest to god real tear trickles down her cheek and she says,

I guess I don't have any right to know anything about you, do I?

No, you don't.

Give me something to remember, she says.

I wear a size eleven boot, I say.

You are so cruel. You really like to hurt me.

Okay. Here's something to remember. When I was a kid I watched my parents drown in the Columbia River. There was a boat wreck, a lot of fire and they burned up and I watched it happen.

Oh, she says. I was thinking of something like a phone number.

I've never gotten married. I live alone. I drive a BMW 850 CSi that's fourteen years old.

Are you making this up? She asks.

I don't write fiction.

She looks professional now, in her uniform and her done hair. Her wide hips, her pointed high heels, her long nails.

I'll dream about you, I say. Is that a consolation?

Sure, she says. For about ten seconds.

You know the rules, Yosanda. You've played the game. How old is he?

Who?

The man you're running from.

Older than you.

She looks at herself in the mirror over the lowboy where a bottle of champagne rests on its side beside an ice bucket and silver chafing dishes stacked up like dead soldiers.

She touches her hair with her left hand and I see the flash of the platinum band, the glitter of the brilliant and I let her go. The space between us opens up to six miles, a distance that grows to infinity and it's like she was never beside me and I was never inside her and that emptiness eats my guts out and I'm standing on the deck of the house on the bluff over looking the Yakima River watching a woman lounge on a deck chair in the sun and she has flaming red hair and freckles on her skin and long legs that beg to be kissed and wide rich hips, and full breasts that strain against her green bikini with its little spaghetti strings that somehow hold it to her.

Well, she says. I guess that's that.

Yeah, I say. Guess so.

The words hover over the gap, then drop forever into the bottomless pit. I feel like a worm has burrowed inside me and I wonder if it's eating my moral fiber right now, getting even with her, shutting her down the way you shut down a car engine when it blows a rod.

So, she says, I have a plane to catch.

Okay.

That's it?

That's it. Tell you what though. If you had red hair, you'd be perfect.

So she has red hair, this woman you're running from?

She opens the closet door, picks out a suitcase that hasn't been opened in three days and two nights. scoops up her purse, slings it over her shoulder and leaves the room.

I lie on the bed feeling nothing.

The House on the Bluff

Leaving the BMW in the sun, I hoist the box holding the granite samples and stand at the gate watching her. A wet footprint on the deck as she rises from the pool dripping, hair dark as blood, skin glittering with those small water diamonds that collect on oiled skin and run in silver streaks down her arms, down her thighs, down her back. She slips into one of her emerald green cheomsangs and shakes her head and the footprint on the pool deck dries up and she sits on the deck chair, knees together, toweling at the pool-wet hair.

Unaware of me there waiting at the edge.

The woman in Reno, on the bed, skin shimmering in the light. She crosses her ankles, the cheomsang slides open from knee to thigh. *The woman in Reno, on her belly, hands clutching the pillow, tense, then letting go, a howl like a wild animal in agony.*

I shove the gate open, feet heavy as concrete boots, clumsy, walking across the deck. She follows me, then lowers the dark glasses.

A smile.

Berle, she says.

She pats the open chair beside her. On the deck beneath her chair, a small pool of water hides in the shadow of her body. She lays back in the chair, hands folded across her flat belly. Skin hidden under the silky cheomsang. *The woman in Reno...her name? can't recall her name right now...starts with a...starts with a...*

Just got a minute, I say.

Where have you been? She says, looking away. I'm not there. A body in space drifting away. No meaning. No purpose.

Reno, I say. A little vacation.

Charlie's working you that hard? She asks.

I brought the granite samples for you to check out.

Any color but red, she says. I hate red.

I don't say she must hate her hair, hate her freckles, hate the polish on her spiked fingernails. She reaches for a bottle of sunscreen, squeezes a white smear from the container into the palm of her hand and wipes it over her thighs and belly, leaning forward to her ankles. *The woman in Reno, kneeling on the floor, arms spread out on the bed, hips thrusting back into my hips, tensing, then that inevitable collapse.* I say,

Yeah, Charlie said stay away from red.

I can't stand red, she says. Nothing red.

Got it, I say.

I open the box. She works in the sunscreen.

I lay out the blue granite slice on the white deck table. In the sun the flecks of feldspar glitter, small stars in the dark blue stone, alive, little insects frozen in time, locked up and bound forever in their small crystalline cells. She says,

I like that.

It's from Wyoming,

I slide the green slice with its dark green streaks of olivine and the black veins that throb in the sunlight—stone blood congealed from wounds six hundred million years old. Maxine says,

Oh, I really like that one.

The yellow granite, rare as dinosaur eggs, against the white table to shimmers like its own stars are streaking out and Maxine fingers the stone, its smooth sawn surface mirroring her fingers. I say,

That's from Upstate New York. Only one quarry does that kind of stone. Very expensive.

She glances at me. I see myself in her glasses—a small man crawling on the lenses waiting for her to squish me. She smiles.

The green one? She says, Where does that come from, Mr. Geologist?

Arkansas, I say.

How do you know so much about granite?

I pick up the stone, turn it over and point at the label—Arkansan Foam, it says in small letter. She says,

Oh. So you don't know anything about granite?

Only what I read, I say.

Well, she says. I like the yellow. I like the blue but I don't want to buy anything from Arkansas for my kitchen.

The New York stone is good, I say. Doesn't fracture.

Why is that good?

They can cut longer pieces, tighter joints.

Which one is the most expensive?

She runs her fingers over all three slices and I want to be the stone. But I just watch her fingertips and then she looks up at me again. Catching my breath, I say,

There's one more sample.

I pluck the last stone from the box, lay it out. It is smooth, pure onyx, the color of anthracite. There's not a fleck of color in it but the sun blisters its skin and Maxine lowers her dark glasses and I gaze at her emerald eyes flicking from my eyes to the stone in a slow, deliberate rhythm.

This one, I say. It's rare. Far as I can tell, it's the purest granite anywhere. You can see—no intrusions.

Intrusions?

Like the olivine and the feldspar. Those little flecks and streaks.

I like that. Purity.

Well, this one, just for the countertop will cost more than the pool and the deck. If you want...

Have you shown these to Charlie?

Haven't seen him today. These just came in.

She stands. The cheomsang swirls around her, the thigh slit, the skin taking the sun and on the skin the freckles cluster like rubies, glistening, and then the silk settles from its storm. She says,

Did Charlie tell you I want to go into Seattle Monday?

Nope.

I stack the samples back into the box, leaving the black granite on the table.

I lost my license, she says.

You can get a replacement at the DMV.

Lost it as in revoked.

Sorry.

That's the problem with this company. Nobody talks to anyone. Monday. I need to be in Seattle and I want you to drive me.

I'll talk to Charlie, I say.

I'll talk to Charlie, she says. Eight A.M. Here. Monday. I want the black.

Okay, I say, but it'll be dark. I'll have to get the architect to rethink the lighting and windows 'cause you don't want a black hole.

I don't care, she says. It's the most expensive, that's what I want.

Then that's what you'll get, I say. Black will take longer. Only one place cuts it. There's a back log.

Shit, she says. She smiles. Raises an index finger to her lips like she wants to flick away a crumb of bread. *The woman in Reno...Yosanda...linen...black hair...lips full and ripe...running from her older husband...woman on the run.* I watch her lips.

She strips off the shades, drops the cheomsang, kicks off the clogs and stands in the sun, the bikini a green mist against her skin, the small pooch of her belly soft as a mound of whipped cream, the hips a little bit thick, the thighs with small dimples.

Walking to the edge of the pool, she settles into the water and dips down, comes back up hair wet again, flaming wet again and she looks at me, rakes me up and down. She says,

I see why he likes you. You're vanilla ice cream.

What? Vanilla?

Vanilla, she says. Vanilla's all right but it needs nuts and chocolate sauce to spice it up.

Do you like vanilla? I say.

But she's under water and her hair snakes out behind her and I turn, pick up the sample box and walk back to the gate, back to the BMW that I know will be as hot as a sauna.

Charlie

It is hot and all I can think about was that slab of black granite and how she ran her fingers over it like it was alive. In the heat, I sweat but it's not the heat making me break out, it's the echo of her laugh. Vanilla, she'd said, vanilla ice cream. Wet, her hair snaked down around her shoulders. He likes you 'cause you're vanilla. *The woman in Reno didn't think I was vanilla.*

I drive from the house on the bluff to the batch plant, down the hill, a hill of river rock cut through with a graded road from the highway to the river bank and beside me, in the BMW 850, the granite slices rattle each one has her fingerprints on it.

At the gate to the plant, I pull up as a mixer truck hauls up and I wave and the driver rolls down the window of his air-conditioned cab and yells,

Hey Berle, welcome back. Dija get laid?

In front of the office Charlie's Lincoln Town Car glistens in its metallic silver skin—like Charlie—a sweaty beast with four black paws. The BMW in its own class outshines the Lincoln.

Charlie McGraw sits at his desk in his big office chair that creaks when he moves. He has a phone glued to his ear. He grunts at me and gives me the one minute sign with his index finger. I set the box of granite on the desk and sit down. Charlie says,

Yeah, we can do that, but it'll cost you extra.

He hangs up and shakes his head.

Guy wants pink concrete for his pool deck.

He laughs he waves a hairy paw at the end of a hairy arm that's growing out of a thick hairy shoulder attached to a XXXL hairy chest wrapped in a XL white shirt open down to the belly button. A gold chain thick as bridge cable drapes around his thick neck. He says,

Welcome back. Did you get laid?

Why's everybody worried about my sex life?

With broad fingers Charlies wipes at the sweat on his half-bald head and he says,

Christ, it gets any hotter I'm gonna build a fucking pool right here. Did you talk to Maxine?

I talked to her. Showed her the samples. She wants the black.

That woman, he says. She's gonna bankrupt me yet.

She said something about driving to Seattle Monday.

Yeah. She lost her license and I got to be in Wenatchee on Monday. Can you handle it?

We have the foundation at the mall in Richland Monday.

Billy can handle that.

What if Billy drives her into the city?

Charlie looks at me. Wipes at his bald head tanned the color of dyed leather and scored with sunspots. He says,

I don't trust Billy. I want you to take her.

How'd she lose her license?

Three speeding tickets in a month. Swear to god her right foot's made outta lead. But you can't hold down a fast woman like that.

The phone jingles and Charlie raises his finger in his one minute sign and answers,

McGraw Concrete, Charlie.

On the drafting table the plans for the new house on the bluff lay spread out. The pool is shaped like a big kidney. I remember Maxine on the deck in her white chair holding the slice of Green Foam granite against the lime green cheomsang stretched across her belly. The bikini is one tick from a misdemeanor and I take a deep breath. Shoulda stayed in Reno, shoulda got on a plane to Atlantic City, shoulda moved away and never come back. Charlie says,

Just a minute. I'll ask him. Berle, can you run into Yakima this afternoon?

I don't say Sure anything that'll get me away from her, get her out of my mind, get that lime green bikini and that flame red hair to disappear and leave me alone. I do say,

What's up?

Guy decided he wants a bid on that apartment complex on Forty-fifth.

Charlie scribbles an address, a name, a phone number on a piece of letter head and shoves it at me and I say,

You know that pool's gonna set you back.

I know, he says. But I wanna keep her happy....

He looks at me, a half-grin on his thick lips. He says in a half-voice,

Woman's got more needs than a houseful of orphans.

I pick up the paper and pocket it and Charlie says,

She wants black granite in the kitchen?

I told her we'd have to change the windows or it'll be dark as a graveyard in there.

She likes dark, he says.

He sits in his big squeaky chair and runs his hairy hand over his face and shakes his head and he scoots the box of granite samples across the desk. He says,

You'll get on that apartment today, right?

I'm on it.

*****

The batch plant orange glows like a setting sun. On the side of the main hopper I read McGraw Concrete and Finishing, Serving the Valley since 1990.

The BMW is hot. The seat hot. The wheel hot. The dash hot. Sitting there, I peek at the address of the apartment house in Yakima and my cell phone chimes and I answer,

Yeah.

It's Maxine, she says.

Yeah, Maxine, What's up?

I changed my mind.

About what?

The black.

You don't want the black.

I don't know if I don't want the black, but I want to see those other samples again.

What changed your mind?

I'm in the kitchen. You're right. It'll be dark with black granite everywhere.

I'll tell Charlie.

Where are you?

On the road to town.

Bring the samples.

Samples are in the office.

So he's got you working already?

Working already, I say.

I see her in the pool, floating like a red flower on clear blue water and I take a deep breath. Shoulda stayed in Reno a week longer, shoulda shoulda stayed away.

Berle?

Yeah?

I just talked to Charlie about Monday. Are you all right with Monday?

Yeah. He told me about your license.

I hope you don't mind.

It's okay, I say.

I hang up the cell, feel the heat of the steering wheel on my palms, feel the sweat trickle down my sides. Sweat means trouble. I remember the woman in Reno in her white suit with the light gray blouse and her black high heels and she's mud wrestling with Maxine and the white suit turns brown and the green bikini slips off Maxine and the halter top covering her slides free and Maxine wraps her legs around my head and I taste her and it's not mud on my tongue.

Monday Morning Maxine

Breakfast—coffee, toast half-burnt, eggs scrambled and scorched.

Bad start.

It's hot early.

The air heavy

It will get worse.

Monday. Time. 6:30 A.M. Leave the A/C on? Turn it off? I stack the cup, plate with toast and eggs and skillet in the sink. Let it soak off the burn.

Gone all day so I shut down the A/C and it dies that slow mechanical wheeze of machines strangling on heat. Right away, sweat pops out under my arm pits.

*****

The BMW. Already blistering in the sun, her black skin reflects light. Should have put her in the garage. Stupid. Even at rest she looks like she just broke the sound barrier—sleek, low, ground hugging without a spoiler to nail her in place.

I glide into the smell of hot leather smothered in a cage. I crank her over, listen to the sound of the mill with the door still open as she comes alive—even with 116,000 miles on the engine she runs as smooth as the day they rolled her off the line in Munich.

Time. 6:40. I ease the BMW onto the street—feels good, that urgency waiting. I hold back, let her lope until she's at operating temperature then I punch it—the thrust rams my head back into the head rest as the blower kicks in and the white line of the highway streaks into a solid pearly ribbon. Have to back down, tastes good, so early, better than scorched scrambled eggs. Six minutes to Maxine.

*****

From the top of the curved black-topped drive, I see Maxine in the sunlight, back-lit, her hair a cascading shower of blood over her shoulders. She wears green framed sunglasses, an emerald green skirt cut to the knee, black stockings and green high heels that would cripple a horse. She carries a big black sack purse slung over her left shoulder. She stands, one hip cocked like a car hop carrying a heavy load.

I stop, lean across the seat and open the door. As she slides in she says,

You're late.

I burned my toast, I say.

She smells of lipstick and lotion and under the cinnamon scent of carnation there is the faint odor of cigarette smoke. She crosses her legs, drops the sack purse on the floorboard and leans back.

Is everything all right? I say.

Charlie. That son of a bitch, never knows when to let well enough alone.

Anything I can do?

I look at her. She looks at me. Draws down the sunglasses. I see her green eyes with gold flecks in the irises. Her lashes are dark, her eye shadow a faint glittery green and her brows are accent lines penciled on her freckled skin.

I don't know. Is there something you can do?

I glance at her. She says,

What are you waiting for?

Seat belt.

Fuck the seat belt, she says.

This vehicle doesn't run with you in a seat without a seat belt.

She draws the strap across her chest and snaps it in place and then she looks at me and smiles. She says,

Satisfied?

*****

I-82 connects to I-90 just outside of Ellensburg. I hit the merge and roll onto I-90. Low traffic beyond a string of semis heading to the pass. I accelerate to eighty, hold it there.

Silence. Then,

You mind if I smoke? She says.

Crack a window.

Wind will fuck up my hair, she says.

She reaches into her sack purse, pulls out a Slim, shakes one loose from the pack and tosses the pack on the dash. I watch her moves, almost rote, a ritual. The cigarette toss, the green lighter, the first drag, the smoke. I tap the button on the console and the window slides down and the smoke flits out, a ghost on the run. A strand of her hair breaks loose and flickers in the stream. A red flag.

Where in Seattle? I say.

Not to Seattle, she says.

What?

How about Yellowstone? He won't think to look for us there.

What are you talking about, Maxine?

You know what I'm talking about. Charlie.

I slow down, pull into the right lane behind a Home Depot semi.

What's going on?

You like working with Charlie?

He treats me right.

You're the only one.

What do you mean by that?

You're a detail man, aren't you?

The dollar's in the details.

You still don't know what I'm talking about, do you?

She lays her left hand on my hand on the wheel and the palm is warm and soft. She says,

If you don't know what I'm talking about, then turn this shitcan around and take me back to the hairy man.

She lets go of my hand. I feel her warmth like a blister. Ahead I see the exit for Cle Ellum. Half a mile. I back down, look at her, she's staring at me her emerald eyes viper-flicking. The exit slips past and Maxine takes a deep breath and she lays her hand on my thigh and she leans close and she whispers,

You do know what I'm talking about.

I hit the accelerator and the 850's blower kicks in and I'm breathing like I've run a mile and my head's whirling. I glance at her hand on my thigh, glance at the bright red nails, the long, spiked nails. I say,

What's the deal here?

He thinks you're vanilla, she says. I don't think you're vanilla. I think you've got more balls than a bowling alley. I need someone like you because I'm sick of Charlie, sick of his bullshit, sick of his hairy paws all over me and you're going to help me get away. Aren't you?

I pass the Home Depot semi and Maxine lifts her hand from my leg and only then do I feel how ready I am, how crazy, stupid, weird and it's like someone opened the dream package and the woman on the chaise longue on the pool deck has stepped out and walked into my brain and it's like everything is happening all at once. She crushes her cigarette in the ashtray that hasn't had a butt in it since the day I bought it. She says,

When you run off to Reno, what do you do?

I gamble, drink.

What else?

What do you think?

Berle, look at you. You live alone, you don't have any lady friends, you drive this piece of junk and you never even once made a move on me even when I was hanging out like an Eats sign at a roadside café.

You think I'm gay.

Are you? Do you go to Reno looking for boys? Pretty boys? Trans? What do you like, Berle? What do you do with all the money Charlie pays you?

He won't be paying me much longer now will he?

He doesn't have to know a thing.

What are you suggesting, Maxine?

I pull off at the summit, lay into the parking lot at the Summit Inn. Maxine looks worried. She says,

What are you doing?

Like you said, I'm a detail man.

Oh for christ's sake, Berle. What do you think? I'm leaving Charlie. A blind man could feel that with his cane. Are you blind?

I can't do that, I say.

Do what?

Help you.

You can because you want to. I see the way you look at me, Berle. A woman can feel that. She doesn't have to be told. That's why I chose you.

You just signed my death warrant then, I say.

I roll down the window. Heat rolls in. She leans back in the seat of the BMW and closes her eyes. Quiet, unmoving. I watch her breathe, chest rising and falling, beads of sweat on her freckled chest. Hands on her thighs, she rubs them up and down, the scratch of her fingers on the nylons is like the slow rattle of a snake crawling through dry leaves. Then she rolls her head to the side and looks at me and in the eyes there is the purest longing I've ever seen in the eyes of a woman and her hair, wispy and wiry trembles, and I lean close to her and taste her lips for the first time and she relaxes into the seat and her hands caress my face as she slips her tongue into my mouth.

Maxine Scares the Devil Out of Berle

Table. Summit Inn.

Head bowed, staring at her hands spread on the fake-wood vinyl tabletop. The backs of her hands so tanned the skin looks red in the neon lights of the café.

I've seen that bowed head before. Shame, someone said, looks down, fear looks around, confidence looks straight ahead. She's ashamed and she twists the napkin into a tight tube and lays it on the plate with the remains of a tuna salad sandwich. She says,

You think I'm pathetic, don't you?

I don't think anything.

I owe you an explanation, I guess.

You don't owe me anything.

Don't you want to know why I have to leave Charlie?

I told you, I don't need to know anything.

God damn it, I'm trying to tell you something and you go all stupid on me...

I study her face, anguished, the lips light red, the eyes dark with shadow, the cheeks flushed so each freckle—a red hot dot on her skin—stands out. If I can connect the dots, I'll see the truth in her past. I say,

What do you want to tell me?

Fuck you, she says.

Maxine, this is all happening pretty fast and I don't have a blueprint.

I forget. You're the detail man, she says. See the details, you see the design, right?

Right.

Okay. When I was six, we lived in a car. My mother worked at Dairy Queen nights and she'd park the station wagon behind the DQ and I'd sleep while she worked. My dad left her when I was four and he left her without anything but me and that station wagon. I don't know where he went or if he's dead but I hope he is.

I don't need to know this.

I need you to know it, she says. I need you to be part of this because I'm making a huge investment here.

Turn around, I say. Go back to Charlie, back to Yakima.

And die?

She opens the big sack purse beside her on the bench and she pulls out stacks of hundred-dollar bills and with each stack she looks at me like each one is a down payment on happiness. There are ten of them, each one with a red rubber band around it. Sweat breaks out under my arms, sweat drips down my neck, the palms of my hands go slick and hot. I say,

What's this?

His blood, she says. His sweat. The way I figure it, every blowjob I gave him was worth ten thousand bucks. Every time he came in my mouth, it costs him twenty grand.

This is not good, Maxine.

Are you worried he'll hunt you down?

I'm not worried about me. I'm worried about you.

I'm not going back, Berle. If you don't want a piece of this, just take me to AmTrak and you're free.

Twice, I say.

Twice what?

Twice now you give me an out.

Does it seem crazy to you?

She shoves a bundle of hundreds across the table. I say,

Put it away. Just put it all away.

That's not all, she says. There's a box at General Delivery in Portland with your name on it.

Portland? My name?

I don't take chances, she says. When I commit, I go all the way. I told you a woman knows the look, Berle. Words don't mean a thing but the look says it all. When you were measuring the kitchen for the granite, I watched your eyes. Eyes that take everything in but don't let anything out.

How much? I say.

I'm not going back to him, Berle. Ever.

How much in the box in Portland?

Four hundred fifty thousand.

What did he do to you?

You don't want to know.

I do.

She looks at her hands again and like a machine she stows the stacks of hundreds back in the purse and then she looks at me and her lips tremble and I want to save her, to wipe away all that pain. She says,

Six hundred dollars. I'm eight years old and my mother sells me for six hundred dollars to a man who liked little girls. Six hundred dollars. All my life I've had that hanging over my head. I was worth six hundred dollars.

Tell me what I can do, Maxine.

You stupid fuck, she whispers. I don't want you to do anything. I want you to listen. Just listen. There's nothing you can do, so just listen to me.

Something rages up in me then. A hard spiny thing in my chest and throat. I want to touch her again. I slide out of the booth and in beside her and I wrap her up tight, feel her trembling, She doesn't resist or hold back. She is small and warm and she nestles against me and we fit like we've been together for a long, long time.

She sobs and broken pieces shake off her and drop until there's nothing left to fall. I tip her face up, look at the lips, the eyes, the acres of anguish glittering there. She says,

Shit. I hate it when I leak like this. I don't want to leak.

At the back of my mind, I see Charlie coming at me with an ax. At the back of my mind, I hear six hundred dollars. I want to know more but this isn't the time. I say,

Let's go to Portland.

You're sure?

I'm sure.

She pulls away from me. I wipe the tears from her cheeks with my fingertips. I say,

If I had a cup, I'd save these for you.

Maxine Cranks Berle's Churn

Maxine lights a Slim with her green and silver lighter. I crack the window. She says,

You got me at a weak moment because I hate to sob like baby.

I meant what I said about saving them.

You're a real romantic, Berle, saving a woman's tears.

You know we can never go back.

Oh, I know. He'll find us. He always does.

I feel the noose tighten around my neck. The cigarette smoke chokes me and I imagine a man in the gas chamber holding his breath as the pellet falls. The pain digs into my chest. a fishhook into muscle. I say,

What does that mean?

Charlie's like one of those birds that flies to Argentina in the winter. He homes in on me like that— must be he smells me or something you know the way a salmon knows where home is.

Are you carrying a GPS?

A GPS?

In your purse. Is there a GPS locator in your purse?

There's a cell phone in my purse.

We'll have to ditch it and get you a pre-paid phone.

We're not ditching my phone, she says. It's got all my numbers in it.

Your friends?

She looks at me and shrugs and takes a long drag on the Slim. I drive thinking about Charlie's reaction to me running off with his woman and I flounder—no roadmap, no guide. What am I doing? I slow down. Maxine says,

Rethinking?

This isn't just about the money?

It's always about the money.

Where does all this end up, Maxine?

Tell me what you were thinking when you measured the kitchen.

You know what I was thinking.

Exactly what you're thinking with that lump in your pants but now you don't have to hide it. I could tell just looking at you that you're a horny stud. So tell me about your little trips to Reno.

I go to Reno, fly back home.

And you get laid, don't you?

I'm a big boy.

I smelled it on you when you were in the kitchen. You can't wash it off, you know. Lust sticks to you like glue.

She scrubs out the Slim in the now not-so-virgin ashtray and I glance at her, at the green skirt, the heels, the blouse open at the neck. She says,

Does it surprise you that I can tell you get laid?

Nothing you do surprises me.

This is going to surprise you, she says.

She rolls up the window sealing out the hum and whine of traffic, the rumble of the highway. Still feeling like I've walked off a cliff, I kick the 850 back up to 75 where it cruises smooth as jello. Maxine says,

When I was twelve, I killed my mother.

I grip the wheel like it's a snake about to strike. It's hot and hard. My foot jiggles on the accelerator. Maxine lays her left hand on my thigh and she whispers,

Easy big boy, you're hyperventilating.

You killed your mother?

You don't believe me? With an ax. Aw, Berle, you're probably thinking what have you gotten into? Right? This crazy bitch killed her mother. When you're twelve, you're just a kid and you know how it is with kids.

We travel in silence, she leaves her hand on my leg, squeezing in a one two three rhythm. She says,

You have to know everything about me or this won't work.

What won't work?

What do you think the money is for? We're going to start over.

Does Charlie know about your mother?

You can't sleep with a man for sixteen years and keep something like that a secret.

She keeps squeezing in that one two three rhythm and I'm lightheaded but I try to keep my eyes on the road and she pretends not to notice. I measure how deep into hell this ticket will take me. I weigh hell against the image of her thighs and the green bikini and the heat of the pool deck where she lay in the sun a sweating goddess and I think about the woman in Reno in her white linen suit and her black hair going back to her husband minus a hundred grand and I wonder if he could smell the lust on her. Maxine says,

My life got pretty sordid from there on.

Okay, tell me. No secrets.

We haven't slept together. Can I save something for later?

I'm already on death row and the clock is ticking so don't hold back. What happened when you were twelve?

What do you mean you're on death row?

You think Charlie won't kill me when he tracks us down? Charlie's not a nice man, Maxine. He's got a mean streak in him wide enough to drive a truck through and we've got...

He found another one, a little thing with blond hair and big hollow eyes that he liked more than he liked me...

He? Who's he? Charlie?

Ted. The man my mother sold me to. Six hundred dollars, remember? So I killed him too and left Emily in the bus station and called the cops because that was the only way I could save her. I don't know what happened to her. When I say it like that it does sound kinda cold, huh?

She lets go of my leg and leans against the door panel and her hair splays out like blood spatter on the glass and light flickers through the curled tresses. I need to touch her so bad my hands shake but I wait, drive in silence, feel the 850 spinning out the miles between us and Yakima and the house on the bluff that now seems like it was a hundred years ago because that's the way it is when you fall through a hole into an alternate universe where everything is upside down. She takes a deep breath. She says,

Are you ready for the next episode in my melodrama?

Six hundred bucks for a sex slave and killing your mother—that's hard to beat.

Oh, it gets better, she says. I was on the street.

At twelve?

I wasn't selling it if that's what you're thinking. I got pregnant.

At twelve?

Fourteen. I'm not HIV positive and I don't have any STDs that I know of. I got raped by four assholes who took turns at me in a box car in Eugene then tossed me out on the tracks. You remember the Bhagwan's commune?

Heard of it.

They saved me, she says. One of the converts found me wandering on a highway to hell somewhere in the summer and they took me in, fed me, let me have my baby there.

Charlie knows about all this?

Well, she says, when you sleep with a man long enough there's secrets. I never told him what I just told you. I never told anyone what I just told you. And that's why we're going to Portland.

Who are we going to kill in Portland?

She laughs and she grips my thigh again and my erection that forgot we are dead comes alive and this time Maxine rests her little finger against my groin and falls silent. Perfume. She smells like carnations and cinnamon and cigarette smoke and she sits upright, neck stiff, eyes straight ahead, flexing her legs, crossing and uncrossing them and I know it's just a matter of time until I do what I've been wanting to do but something in me says go slow, make this last as long as you can because it just might be the last time you ever get laid. It's been four hours since we left the house on the bluff overlooking the Yakima River but we've covered a million miles and opened a dozen cans of worms. I look in the rear-view mirror, wonder if the black SUV tailing me is the angel of death. I know Charlie and I know that stealing his money will make him mad and what stealing Maxine will turn him into.

My mouth feels full and I can't swallow the way a man can't when he's got a mouth full of death shouting at him that he shouldn't have done what he did.

Worried? Maxine says.

Just checking traffic.

He won't be onto us for another six hours, she says. You have lots of time to think before you die. You think a lot don't you, Berle? I see you thinking, picking at the details like that GPS thingy, sorting out the details, wondering just what the fuck is going to happen to you, right? Well, did you ever stop to think what would happen if you stopped thinking and forgot about the details and just went with the flow?

Every time I go with the flow I wind up going over a water fall.

You have nice thighs, you know that? Maybe we should go to Cannon Beach so I can bury you in the sand.

I just stole Charlie's woman.

Fuck Charlie. He's had his turn and I'm not his woman and you didn't steal me.

She wiggles her little finger in the crease of my thigh, just a whisper of a touch, but it's enough. I check the mirror again and I see a giant chain saw whirring down the highway attached to the front end of a semi and it's headed right for me. Maxine leans her head against my shoulder and she says,

Just like run-away teenagers, huh Berle?

Outside Looking In

Maxine has this glass shell around her now—she closed it off after the tears, after we left the Summit Inn. Look, smell, don't touch and for the first time since I watched Mom and Dad burn up, I feel something—a small something like a rock slide of big boulders burying me and there's something dangerous about her sitting beside me in the hum and hiss of the 850 hot and purring. I know she's dangerous but pulling away is impossible. I look at her reflection on the windshield, see in her a hazy angel descending but the haze is cigarette smoke and my brain's clouded by her perfume because I want that, I'm hungry for that. Maybe it's because I know I'm a dead man, dead man because when Charlie tracks us down, he'll gut me, draw and quarter me, maybe shoot me in the head and then what? What have I done? I think about Reno, the woman in the white linen suit, that tattoo ringing her thigh, so safe now, no danger there, just three days of sex and steak and shrimp and lobster and champagne. But Maxine wants my soul. Wants all of me. How does she read my mind? Like a gypsy reading palms, she nails me.

The struts of the Fremont Bridge over the Columbia flash by, green struts, steel trees holding up the sky. She says,

You're too quiet, Berle.

I'm thinking, I say.

You shouldn't think. You're not good at it.

I got you here, now what?

Downtown, she says. The Franklin Hotel.

She lays her long fingers, polished red as the fire of hell on my leg and she says,

It's just across from the post office.

I take the downtown exit from I-5, cross lanes of traffic. Haven't been in Portland for a while, used to come to Portland when I was sane, before I saw her on the pool deck, before that red hair drove me crazy, before I saw her in a green bikini, before I smelled her body and its wild animal scent. I roll through the streets, four o'clock thick with sane men on their way home, sane men with jobs, sane men driving sane cars, sane men with sane wives and sane kids watching TV. I make a left on Lovejoy Street and pull into a slot in front of the Franklin Hotel, across the street from the post office. Maxine says,

What time is it?

I glance at the dash clock right in front of her and it says half-past crazy and she's got her eyes on me, watching me, not the clock and she squeezes my thigh and whispers,

It'll be all right, Berle. I'll stay here, you go get your package.

Her teeth are smile-white, her lips kiss-me red, her eyes fatal-green. I lean into her, take the mouth, take the warm red lips. She holds steady, doesn't offer more. I pull away. She says,

Go get your package.

The post office is a Neo-Fascist behemoth with medallions stuck to it and eagles escaping from it. It's an insult to architecture, a left-over from another time when square and thick was the norm—thick like me—thick and square and stupid and crazy as a room full of bats.

An old-fashioned building, it needs a body transplant to bring it into the 21st century. Inside, it smells like floor wax and that peculiar stuffy smell of dying buildings with thick walls and no air conditioning and windowsills where no dust ever accumulates. At the window, I ask the clerk— a woman with orange hair and black lashes so thick they make her eyelids droop—for my package. Berle Kubiak. General delivery.

ID? She says.

I tug out the billfold, pull the license from its plasticine window. She studies me, then the photo. She says,

Washington, huh?

Yeah. Here on vacation.

Yeah, she says.

She comes back carrying a box the size of a laptop computer wrapped in brown paper and taped tight. She slips the box across the countertop. So this is what four hundred and fifty-thousand dollars feel like.

Back across the street, I dodge cars and a streetcar and slide into the 850 where Maxine sits, hands folded in her lap, looking like a Madonna on the Rocks. All that's missing is the fifth of scotch. She smiles. She says,

How does it feel?

How does death feel?

You worry too much.

I lay the box in her lap. Perching her hands on the box, she closes her knees.

Aren't you curious? She says.

No.

Not even a little bit?

All right. I'm curious, but I can wait.

The room is in your name, too, she says.

You thought of everything. Did you think of where to bury me?

You're such a worry wort.

MAXINE

*****

The foyer of the Franklin Hotel is gray marble with sky blue drapes. The front desk is art deco mahogany and the furniture is art deco spare and lean and the desk clerk is a young boy with a shiny angelic face and a pointed chin like a dart aimed at his heart. He has black hair, slicked back and glistening, and he has the darkest bags under his eyes I've ever seen. I say,

You've got a room for Berle Kubiak.

He nods. I watch his hands, delicate androgynous hands, the nails lacquered, the skin smooth as chamois. No rings. Only the black band of a silver watch. He lays a key on the desk. Room Three Sixteen. It's an old-fashioned key that will fit an old-fashioned lock in an old-fashioned door that will have geometric woodwork on it and be painted sky blue like the drapes.

The register is an old-fashioned book with a leatherette cover you used to see on a bookkeeper's desk. The pages are green, the lines are black, and there are fresh names in the book so the Franklin Hotel is a hot bed of something illegal or desirable or clandestine.

Maxine at the door, stands as far from me as she can get and still be in the room. She holds her sack purse and the brown paper package and she shines. I get a surge in my groin, desire looking for a way to break out and I think about the woman in Reno talking about me—you save it up, she said, then you let the dam burst here.

I leave the desk, the clerk stops me.

Sir? Mr. Kubiak?

I listen to his voice, high and clear like a teen-age girl. I turn back to him.

I'll need to swipe your card, sir.

You take credit cards?

We're very modern, he says.

He licks his red lips and bats his lashes in a way you never get used to.

I walk to the elevator. Maxine follows like we're strangers.

Double Occupancy

Maxine leans against the wall of the elevator her eyes distant, clutching the sack purse big as a suitcase under her left arm, the box with my name on it under her right. The elevator—burnished brass—dings for floor three and the door opens and Maxine shuffles out.

The hallway is silent. The carpet blue. Big art deco vases perch on art deco glass-topped stands and art deco mirrors hang on the blue papered walls.

Room Three Sixteen is halfway down the hallway. I open the door. Maxine hangs back. My paranoia already running in high gear, I glance left and right as the door opens. Maxine enters like a shadow gracing the big well lighted room that has the feel of a story book place an antiques dealer bought and forgot about. I remember the hotel room in Reno—a thousand years ago—where the surfaces were hard and flat so the maid could wash sin off with a sponge and mop up moral decay with bleach. Maxine turns to me. Her face is calm, her eyes liquid. I say,

So here we are in the joint of no return.

You can go, she says. Just walk out the door.

I glance at the door. It is blue, wood, with stylized flowers framing it. Art deco craftsmanship done with care and pride. The kind of work that takes time, the kind of work that collects dust and needs a full-time maid to keep it shiny and clean.

Maxine settles on the big double bed with a flared wooden art deco headboard. The sack purse beside her. She lays the brown paper wrapped box on the blue bed spread. I kneel, facing Maxine. She reaches for my face and her hands are cool, smooth. She whispers,

If you need to go, go ahead.

I don't need to go.

I'll be fine.

I need to know what you want.

What I need is right here, she says.

She strokes my cheek. I want to kiss her but there are too many questions I don't have answers for. I say,

Now what?

Always the detail man?

Details make the story.

First thing, she says, is to get you some clothes.

I laugh. Clothes. That's not what I need. I need to know what's driving this whole thing and why and where and who's to blame for whatever goes wrong. I go check out the bathroom where twin white terry cloth robes hang on the wall beside a bathtub that looks like a cube of white marble. An elegant gold shower head arched like a swan's neck hangs from the wall. Art deco faucet handles in polished brass, the kind they don't make anymore. I look back at Maxine on the bed, her legs crossed, her left foot bouncing. She's dropped her high heels and her legs shimmer in the light. She has lit a Slim and the smoke is a cloud around her head. I say,

What happens if I leave you here?

Is that what you want?

I'm lost.

She takes a drag on her Slim, exhales, the smoke coiling around her. She says,

Is this how you thought it would be?

I didn't think about how it would be.

While you were in Reno, did you think about me while you were getting laid.

What do you think?

I think you thought about me and that's why you didn't hesitate when I gave you the chance to run.

I don't really think.

Then walk out that door.

You're right. I thought about you, but this isn't like I thought it would be.

Did you dream up so overblown fantasy about me? Did you think Charlie would go away and leave us together? Is that what you thought? Come here, take off my blouse.

There's a rap on the door. Maxine stands, her Slim gripped between her fingers. She looks at me. She says,

So soon? Fuck.

Go to the bathroom, shut the door.

The rapping comes again, harder this time. Maxine flits away in a cloud of smoke. I wait till she's gone and then crack the door. The desk clerk with the black bags under his eyes stands there, a half smile on his smooth baby face. I say,

Yeah?

Is everything all right, Mr. Kubiak?

Yeah. It's all right.

He shuffles his feet, wipes at his face with his long delicate fingers with the lacquered nails and he smiles. He says,

We have a house rule, Mr. Kubiak.

And that is?

He glances over my shoulder. I know the sack purse is on the bed and the brown paper package is beside it and Maxine's high heels are on the floor. He blinks those black eyes with the heavy lashes. He smiles again.

It's the room, he says. Single occupancy, sir.

What is that supposed to mean.

He bats his eye lashes again, the slow flirty batting of a young girl winking at her soon to be lover and he says,

Nothing, sir, but it is single occupancy.

The bathroom door opens. Maxine's coming out of the bathroom and she's wearing one of the terry cloth robes and her hair is done up in a white towel and she says,

What is it, Berle?

The single occupancy rule, I say.

The clerk smiles. Maxine closes in on us, wraps an arm around my waist, snuggles close to me. She says,

Invite him in, honey. It might be fun for you.

Maxine, I say.

She breaks loose. The clerk shrinks like a flower drying in the sun. I say,

Okay. I'll come down and fix it.

I'm sorry, the clerk says. I thought she...

Are you coming in or not? Maxine says.

The clerk looks at me, a question on his face a mile wide and he wipes his hands on his thighs but he backs out into the middle of the hallway. I follow, room key in hand. I force him against the wall. I say,

She's with me. That's what she is. You see?

Yes sir, he says. I thought.

You thought she was a hooker, right?

It is single occupancy, sir.

I follow him to the exit door, walk behind him down the steel stairs that echo with each footstep. At the door to the foyer, the clerk stops, turns to face me. He clears his throat, hand on the doorknob. He says,

She didn't mean that, did she sir? About inviting me in. I don't....

I lay a hand on his shoulder, squeeze hard. He shrinks under the pain and shoves the door open.

Swimming in Hundreds

The room is quiet and hot. Maxine kneels on the bed, her back to me, the white terry cloth robe flared around her, the brown paper package open on the floor beside the bed.

I watch as she cracks open a bundle of hundreds and lays them out one at a time where already a river of green floods from the headboard to the foot of the bed. In the package, there are still bundles unopened, rubber bands still tight around them.

Maxine turns to look at me over her shoulder, her hair hiding half her face, a siren in a pinup. And it works. But I'm easy. She says,

You're alone.

It's all straightened out.

You need money?

That kid thought you were serious.

He was cute in his little girl way.

She pats the bed, bills flutter off the spread like green insects. She says,

Sit, let's play house. I'll be the mama, you be the naughty little boy.

I sit beside her, smell her perfume now boiling off her body. I notice that her hands tremble as she plucks a hundred from the stack and lays it out, follows it with another one counting one hundred, two hundred, three hundred, four. I see where she's going and I reach for her hand to stop her but she shrugs me away and lays the sixth hundred down and she says,

Six hundred. That's what I'm worth.

No, No.

My mother was a junkie, she says. And a whore who sold her body without a second thought. And then, to get what she needed, she sold me too.

Her voice cracks. She sobs and I touch her and this time she melts against me, hot and sweet smelling. She weeps letting it out in small bursts like blood surging with each heartbeat.

Shit, she says. It's always right there, isn't it? When you don't expect it, it pops out and bites you.

She wipes at her eyes with the back of her hand. Her eye liner smears into a hollow-eyed mask with a bright red gash of a mouth. She licks her lips. I lean into her and kiss her and she lays back on the bed, on the hundreds, a white flower on a green field.

I hate it that you're wounded, I say.

You know there's more to the story, right?

I lie down beside her, the first time I've ever curled up with four hundred and fifty thousand dollars. She says,

You're a strange one, Berle Kubiak. And I have a problem with you. I'm half naked, lying on this bed, you've still got your pants on, and you kiss me like I'm your little sister.

I never had a little sister, I say.

She pulls loose, sits up, straddles me and holding my arms out like the crucified criminal she looks into my eyes.

Don't you want me?

I thought we settled that back at the Summit Inn. I'm here. You're here. We've got Charlie's money. The question is where do we go now?

I killed her, she says. You understand what kill means?

She watches my eyes. I watch the robe open. She's bare from her chin to as far down as I can see and as far as I can see it's worth a lot more than six hundred bucks. She says,

Nothing? I tell you I killed my mother and you don't say a thing.

She waits for me to be shocked. I watch her breasts rise and fall with each breath. I remember her on the pool deck in the sun in a bikini and I try to think how a little patch of spandex with two little strings could hide all of what I'm looking at.

And Charlie knows this?

Oh yeah. He knows it.

It's my turn to pull free. She rolls off, onto her knees, sits looking at me. I lean against the headboard and the hundreds slip and slide like grease chunks under me. She doesn't adjust the robe.

This guy who bought you?

Ted. I lived with him for two years. He taught me how to fuck. When I started to pube, he bought another one. He was going to toss me out so I killed him too.

Another one? You mean another girl?

You don't believe me, do you? You think I'm making this up. You think I want you to feel sorry for me.

Well, I say. You did steal half a million dollars from your husband and we have to talk about that sometime.

I never married Charlie.

Her face twists up then like the pain has hit her hard. Her mouth trembles, her hands shake and she swipes at the bills on the bed sending them flying in a green rain. She whimpers as the shell cracks and the tears seep out of her eyes. I take her hands, pull her to me and wait.

When the break is that wide, all you can do is wait. Wait for the blood to clot, wait for the heart to pull itself back into the chest, wait for the tears to stop if they ever do stop. She lies still and quiet against me. The white robe askew baring parts of her in a tempting delicatessen and of course I want to touch, but there's time. I remember Reno— two days and three nights but that was sex and this is something else. I don't know quite what it is, but it's something I haven't felt before. I've burned every bridge back to Charlie. I don't have a job. My house is empty, my bank account is loaded. My car has a tank full of gas but my moral index has sunk to zero. And I still don't know what it is.

Maxine whispers into my ear,

I left her at the bus station in Eugene.

I hesitate. I'm in that place when you really want something, but you're edgy about taking it because the offer might be a trap and when it springs, you're lost, legs broken, neck snapped, fingers crushed, chest caved in, skull shattered but you're waiting for the right time to tell her you're broken as bad as she is and if you touch her, you might be the trap, the swamp that swallows her and so you hold back, watching her, watching the money on the bed, watch her watch you watch her and you see the fear in her eyes, those green eyes shining as bright as a viper's fixed on you and they say come on—Take the plunge, drop through the trap door and feel me because I'm real and everything you're hiding from is right here too.

Maxine says, Backing out?

I've been here before.

You've never been here before.

All this. The way you are, the robe, the bed.

She catches up a wad of hundreds, Charlie McGraw's hundreds and she stacks them neat into a bundle and wraps a rubber band around them and then she says,

What do you mean?

And so I tell her about the woman in Reno, about three nights and two days in a room and I tell her about lobster thermidor and crab cocktails and champagne buckets and a diamond ring. I tell her about the woman who was running from her husband and how I told here that if she had red hair she'd be perfect.

I look at Maxine the way a penitent seeks the eyes of a redeemer and I don't know what to expect but long shiny streaks of tear mar her freckled skin and she reaches across the gulf between us, six inches, a million miles and she touches me and her hand is electric again and her skin is soft and warm.

You told her that? She says. It sounds like you were thinking about me all the time.

All the time, I say. Every second, every minute, every day.

Maxine turns away and she picks at the toenails on her left foot, the white robe parts over her leg, the rest of her covered up, pristine, pure and when she's finished poking at her nails, she glances up at me and she says,

You ate lobster thermidor with her in bed?

I laugh. All the fear is gone, the hesitation gone, the anger and anxiety gone and I say,

Her room, her money.

You are one cheap bastard, Berle Kubiak.

I touch her leg, open the robe. She presses her hand over mine. I stop. Hesitant again. She says,

Did you practice safe sex? Because you didn't just fuck her, you fucked everybody she ever fucked and everybody her no account husband fucked and now you're here with me.

Yeah, I did but there's always a little leakage.

Did you pick her up or did she find you?

I remember watching the woman in Reno with the bald-headed man named Bill. Bill who lasted twenty minutes and who wore a wedding ring but said he wasn't married. I see Maxine's point and I say,

You never know about these things.

Maxine gets off the bed, holding a bundle of hundreds. She stoops and stacks the bundle in the package on the floor and then she walks to the desk and picks up - the phone and dials looking at me, holding me with her gaze. She asks for room service.

I want some lobster thermidor and a bucket of champagne. Well, what the fuck kind of hotel is this if you don't have lobster thermidor. Okay. Cracked crab and French bread then and two green salads and I don't care how much it costs.

Hanging up, she looks at me, legs crossed, foot dancing to a slow rhythm that makes the hem of the robe bounce up and down. She says,

I never thought I'd be jealous of a lobster.

Are you jealous?

Charlie wanted to marry me, but I wasn't going to do that.

Why not?

Because he's too hairy. You've seen him. I like smooth men, like you. All that smooth skin gets to me. Why didn't you ever swim in the pool? I never saw you naked. You got an eyeful of me every time you came over and I didn't hide anything from you because I wanted you to see it, but you...you're like the Virgin Mary all wrapped up in her holiness and hot as a fire cracker but unavailable. Why is that, Berle?

She comes to the bed, sits down and touches my face. Runs her fingers over my beard. Then over my neck.

You'll need a razor, she says, and some clean underwear.

I take her hand, turn it over, palm up, kiss it. Taste the sweat and the perfume and the lotion and I remember watching her crawl out of the pool, hair hanging down like wet red fire, her skin glistening in the sunlight.

Charlie won't let you go so easy.

He thinks I'm in Seattle talking to a lawyer. It'll take him a week before he realizes I'm gone and a month to find me.

So what is this, Maxine? A few days in a hotel room and then what?

Is that what you think?

I don't know what to think.

I chose you, Berle. You know what that means, right?

You might have talked to me first.

I know everything about you, she says. I know how long you've been in that house, I know where you went to school, I know about the fire that killed your folks, I know where you bought that car you drive. Same detective who found my sister checked you out. I see the way you look at me, and I like it. For a year, you were a closed book but then about six months ago, something happened and the book opened and you're looking at me from behind those dark glasses with those radar eyes. You think a woman won't feel that look?

You want to know what happened six months ago?

I want to know.

One day I looked at you out there on that pool deck and I saw you for the first time, really saw you. Maybe it was the way the spaghetti straps on your bikini cut into your skin. Maybe it was the way water ran off your legs when you got out of the pool. Maybe it was the way the sun shimmered when you close your eyes. Sure, but then I read under the skin that you're unhappy and sad and that makes me sad because I feel what you're feeling, but the main thing is this—now that I've helped you steal half a million dollars, where do we go from here?

First we eat the crab, then we go to see my sister. She's all grown up.

How much did you pay the detective?

He came with the lawyer.

How much?

Thirty-thousand dollars.

How much did I cost you?

You were cheap, Berle. It was all in one place. I could have found it myself, but it's better to have a pro dig these things up.

I don't want to eat here, I say. Not in the room, not on the bed.

We'll take it in the dining room then, she says. I'm starved.

She leaves me with the bundles of hundreds. I pick up one, smell it, feel it. The acrid metallic taste of old money filters to my tongue. I listen to her in the bathroom, the sound of water running, her cough, and she shouts,

We have to go to a drugstore. I need a toothbrush and some deodorant.

I leave the bed, walk to the door. I say,

Why didn't you pack a toothbrush?

Charlie would have noticed something like that.

She sends me a mock kiss, pursing her lips and returns to the mirror leaving me to watch her and to think about the hole I'm in and how deep it is and how do I ever get out of it. Do I want to get out?

Maxine finishes. She's back together and the white robe is pooled on the floor and she looks at me and says,

Are you ready?

I follow her to the elevator where she stands back to the wall, lost in time, her sack purse over one shoulder, ankles crossed. I look at the ankles in the high heels and they are trim, bare, tanned, freckled and the harder I look at her in her time of neglect the deeper the hole gets and I know there's only one way out. I want to kiss her, pretend we're strangers, kiss her and when the door opens each go our own way—nothing happened but a memory.

The door opens and an elderly couple with white hair and carrying canes dotters into the car. Maxine and I exit.

Cracked Crab and Sliced Tomatoes

The dining room is white linen on black legged tables resting on plush sky-blue carpeting. The waiter is a tall thin swarthy man with marcelled hair. He wears black shoes, black pants, a white shirt with a black bow tie and a white bolero jacket. His hair glistens. We're in a time warp, we're in an old movie, we've stepped through the looking glass into an alternative universe where I expect to see bug-eyed men with Thompson submachine guns blasting holes in portly men with red carnations in their lapels.

Two for dinner? The waiter says.

We've ordered, I say, cracked crab.

We follow him to a table against a wainscoted wall. Above the wood, light blue panels with bright botanicals. Birds. Flowers. An idyll. An Eden in pastel.

The waiter holds Maxine's chair and she glides into place and I sit across from her studying her. She's coy, patting the silverware, the white napkin. She then looks at me and the light in her eyes dances.

Your order will be right out, the water says. Bowing, he leaves us. Maxine says,

So, is this something you do all the time?

A time or two.

You have a secret life, don't you?

You already know everything about me, I say. We've put it off long enough, Maxine. What happens here, now?

66

She spreads her napkin in her lap, fiddles with the spoon and then she says,

I'd like you to go talk to Emily.

Emily?

Emily, my sister.

Why don't you go to her?

Because I'm ashamed.

Of what?

Who I am, what I did. I can't just waltz into her life like nothing has happened. Christ, Berle, I gave her up. I haven't seen her in 20 years. I mean, she's got to hate me.

This detective who found her, he didn't talk to her.

No.

Why not?

Because he was paid to find her and let me do the rest.

And this is the rest?

This is it.

Why didn't you just tell Charlie what was going on?

Does it matter? Now?

I don't know. But what I do know is that I'm in a big dilemma.

A big word, dilemma, she says. I hope I didn't make a mistake with you.

What do you expect from her? Emily.

I just want to see her again.

Is that what the money is for?

You mean maybe I buy her affections?

I marvel at the intensity in Maxine's face, the set of her jaw. Then, she smiles at me, the face comes bright and clean again. She says,

My mother sold me, Berle. And I hated her for it.

Six hundred dollars, I say. Not a very fair price for such a fair princess.

Emily doesn't have to know anything about the money. What did you say?

What?

Just now. What did you call me?

I don't remember.

You called me a fair princess, didn't you? No one has ever called me princess before.

Now it's my turn to be coy and I'm the one fiddling with the silverware and twisting the napkin like it's the neck of a scrawny chicken.

Do you want out? She says.

I've come this far, I say. Might as well play it out to the end.

Even if the end means you die?

Are you the black widow?

No, but Charlie is a vicious son of a bitch.

The waiter arrives pushing a cart with silver chafing lids on spectacular white plates, a silver wire basket with bread covered with a white cloth, an ice bucket with a bottle of wine, and green salads. He lays it out for us. Pours two glasses of wine, bows, lifts the silver lids from the plates and leaves us alone. Maxine smiles. She says,

Do you hate me?

Let's eat, I say. We'll talk about that later.

The cracked crab has been picked into soft mounds. Thin slices of tomato adorn the edges of the plate. Four black olives are set like jewels around the mounds of crab. On the plate there is a silver container of cocktail sauce. Maxine whispers,

Was the lobster thermidor as elegant as this?

The lobster thermidor was fuel, I say. This is art.

What was she like? Maxine says. The woman in Reno?

Eat your crab.

I need to know. What was she like?

She was screwed up, I say. Anyone who goes to Reno to do what she does is screwed up.

But you liked her, didn't you?

I look at Maxine. Set my fork down.

I'm here with you. I've crossed the Rubicon for you. Nothing on the other side of the river matters now.

Are you going to sell your house? She says.

A Place to Work

Maxine is quiet when we leave the hotel. She leans against the door of the 850 as far from me as she can get. Traffic is smooth, the stop lights easy. I drive with the map on the GPS inching us along southbound to Garden Street where I make a left turn. Maxine unglues herself from the protective shell of the door. I say,

Are you ready for this?

*****

It stinks of bourbon with that thick varnish of sex and cigarette smoke laced with perfume and the sweat of hot bodies working under hot lights and the juiced up scent of head cheese as men, watching women bend their torsos like carnival contortionists, come in their jeans. I've been there, smelled that, seen that look of rapture in the eyes of men thinking about the dancer in front of them, but Maxine, hard as nails, old as sin, looks shocked and dismayed and the grip of her hand on my arm is pure steel.

The music, thick as an animal in heat, the primitive thump driving pelvises left, right, mating music whose outcome is fixed by millions of years of fucking. Light playing on sweaty sequins flash and dart, living creatures sweating out a day's wages and under the smell of sex and under the beat, there hangs the hungry jaws of deception.

It is a special place.

The sawdust floor, red leather stools pushed against a bar. In the mirror, behind the bar, I see a row of faces lined up like skulls with the skin flayed from the bone, reddish death-masks, masks of the dead just waiting for the end of time before falling into their graves.

Oh god, Maxine says.

She clings harder to my arm, her hand hot, vise-like but in her eyes there is the curiosity of innocence watching the devil peel off his skin to reveal the fine structured bones of desire.

It's okay, I say. She's okay. It's just a place to work. But as I say it, I know she isn't okay and it won't ever be okay again because this is the last stop, the last watering hole before the body gives out, the knees can't take the stress, the lungs can't take the smoke, the eyes the dark nights. This is the ruined oasis before all that's left is the top side of a mattress and fifteen bucks dropped on a dresser without a thank you, see you later, don't call me. Maxine says,

Are you sure this is the place?

Umhuh, I say. This is the place.

I watch the lights shift from red to blue to red. These places are always red, so red the skin of the women turns black and exotic then fiery.

Maxine bumps into a cocktail waitress carrying a tray of shots and suds and the waitress turns with the demure coquettishness that only women who live at the mercy of tips possess, but Maxine grips her arm, rattling the shots, and she says,

I'm looking for Emily.

Emily? I don't know any Emily, the waitress says and she slithers through the red light and the smoke swimming through the thump of techno pop that turns the women into pleasure machines grinding in the techno age. Maxine shouts into my ear,

Let's go. This can't be right.

She's here, I say.

I guide Maxine to the bar, to the hefty blonde with the low-cut blouse and the double C cups holding breasts that jiggle as she jerks the draft handle. I lay a ten on the bar as I shout,

Emily? You know Emily?

She glances at the ten, scrapes the head off the schooner of beer, and then looks at me and back at the ten. I peel another bill from the wad in my hand and slide it to her and she smiles and says,

Through the green door at the back.

Maxine has the look of a soul wandering the walled city of Dis and she's still stumbling and crazy and even with my hand on her waist, she hesitates, afraid to go through that door because deep down she knows what she'll find.

I open the door—a thick leather-bound, brass studded door with a brass knob worn black with sweat and oil and the fruitless grasping of women for wealth that vanishes before it closes behind them. I push Maxine through. The door swings shut and with its closing the hollow hammering of the music moans to a quiet throb, and the scent changes from sweat and semen and cigarette smoke to hair spray and lipstick and perfume.

Maxine is shell-shocked.

She freezes like a dog on a chain hitting the limit. I face her. I lift her chin. Peer into her eyes, wet and frightened. She whispers,

What have I done?

You didn't do anything.

Leading her deeper into the back room, I open a door that says Dancers on it and inside there is a row of mirrors and dressing tables and a woman sits at one of the tables and she glances up in the mirror as we enter. I see a heart-shaped face, a face with still-pink skin, rouged, a face with fine lips stained purple, black eyes lined with slashes of purple liner—a mask. I say,

Emily?

She spins on the chair. Faces us.

She surveys us like an explorer discovering a corpse and then she turns back to the mirror and her lipstick and eye liner and she says,

Who wants to know?

I'm not a cop, I say.

I'm not worried, she says.

Emily? Maxine whispers.

You know me, I don't know you, Emily says.

She stands. She is just at five feet but put together with the precision of a body from a factory—perfect fine curved round. Out of place in this place where the women live their last hope hating for the lights to come up, hating that their wrinkles will show under the cracked pancake makeup. Maxine says,

Why do you work here?

Emily faces her. She wears a leopard skin bikini, a push up bra that does her justice, and high heels. She studies Maxine. In her eyes I see a flicker of I know who you are. She lowers a hand to the back of the chair. She wobbles on her heels like she's spaced out and then like two Ferraris clashing at 110 MPH, the two women meet head on and Maxine is sobbing and Emily is saying Oh god.

I stand to one side. Forgotten. Lost. The blood bond in the two women recognizable even after twenty years. Maxine says,

Oh Sweetie, oh sweetie, like she's forgotten the rest of the language and it all comes together in that one phrase, oh sweetie. They are not like twins, but they are near copies of one another. Maxine, red-headed, Emily's hair black as soot. Maxine freckled, Emily smooth, glassy almost polished. They are alike but they are different and there is no doubt they are sisters. Maxine can't speak but her face says it, tear streaked, tense, puckered like a war widow getting the bad news and twenty years of pain dissolve in the salt and the perfume and Emily says,

I was sure you were dead.

What are you doing here? Maxine says.

Wanna eat. Gotta work.

Maxine kisses her and circles her shoulder and she says,

Honey, this is Berle Kubiak. He's saved my life and he knows everything.

We have to talk, Emily says.

You have to quit this place, right now.

I can't.

You can. You will, Maxine says.

She hugs Emily again and then there is a rap on the door and the door opens and a big man with a shaven head leans in and spots me and he says,

Hey shit head, no customers in the dressing room.

It's okay, Carl. He's with my sister.

Sister's gotta go, 'cause you're on babe.

She's not going on tonight, Maxine says.

Oh shit, babe, you can't quit, Carl says.

Maxine says, Get dressed sweetie.

Give me a minute, Carl, Emily says.

You're outa minutes, he says.

And Emily looks at Maxine and she sighs and her bra rises and falls and she says,

I gotta go, Maxine.

I gotta see you again, Maxine says.

You found me here, can you find where I live?

We'll find it, I say.

Emily looks me up and down and the hard stare in her eyes softens and then she slides out the door, her high heels clicking and the door closes behind her and Maxine sags against me and she says,

She's ruined, isn't she, Berle?

*****

From the front seat of his pickup, Clyde watches Maxine get out of the BMW, watches Berle reach for her hand, watches her shrink away and walk into the Franklin Hotel.

Clyde takes off his glasses. They are thick lenses with heavy metal frames and he wipes at his eyes, feeling the weariness of an all-night drive. He tries to figure out what she was doing at the newspaper but he doesn't much care because he has instructions.

He pulls the cell phone from the left front pocket of his plaid shirt, puts his glasses back on, shifts his gimme-cap to one side so the cell phone doesn't bump against it and he calls a number and when it answers he says,

Portland, boss. Hotel Franklin like last time. What do you want me to do?

He waits, listens, shakes his head yes a few times and then he closes the phone.

Silence in the Bedroom

I've watched women go silent hoping quiet will swallow pain. In that dark place, the light's a long way off and the only sound she hears is the rush of blood in her ears as she remeasures the past, weighs her missteps and false starts, revisits her crimes and small sins of omission. In the 850, I smell the remains of her perfume, a thin shell of scent closing her into the torment of her past.

The light changes.

I jerk to a stop when a yellow Mercedes squeals through the red, fishtailing inches from the bumper of the BMW.

Maxine, leaning against the door, hasn't heard death slip by. Two inches more and she wouldn't have anything to atone for.   Inching through the intersection, I find the street with the hotel, park. I can't imagine the tape she's running in her head but I'm sure there's a little girl carrying a white dress and I'm sure the little girl is standing in the restroom of the Greyhound Bus Depot, and I'm sure Maxine swims in a sea of anguish until the little girl disappears. It's the scene she runs over and over, has been running over and over trying to change it, to erase it, to make it stop but it's endless and she's empty and in the quiet of the car I wait until, like a machine switching on, Maxine sits up. She sucks in a deep breath. She whispers,

Where are we, Berle?

At the hotel, I say.

She looks around. Pain etching grooves in her skin. She's still back at the Greyhound hoping it'll all turn out different this time. It won't. It can't. I know it, she knows it. It's what makes us human—living in the hopeless past, seeing the pain of our future.

Maxine lugs her sack purse from the floor like it weighs fifty pounds. She holds it in her lap. Then she glances at me and smiles a smile ripped with anguish so thick and heavy it makes her face sag. She says,

I've lost her.

Maxine looks at me and the pain, if it had claws and fangs, could not tear her any deeper. For a long time she can't breathe then it pours out, twenty years of hurt pulsing out in broken sobs.

*****

For the second time that night, we enter the hotel, step into the art deco innocence of a place trapped in another time, a place where you can go back to the past that never changed. The hotel carrying its time load in the arches and planes of its architect has entered the lost world of the 21st Century where the common denominator is black and the common currency is excess, where the desk clerk on her night shift still wears her hair in a half Mohawk, half peeled to the skull, and she still wears her dangly earrings that point down to the tattoo riding on her breast like a battle ribbon.

I stop at the desk, ask if there's anything for Room Three-Sixteen. She says there was a man looking for us, the same man who showed up earlier. I ask what he wanted. She says she doesn't know but she told him we had checked out. I lay a twenty on the desk and say,

If he comes again, tell him we left an Anchorage forwarding address.

In the elevator Maxine stands vacant eyed like a Roman statue that's lost its paint. I slip in just as the door clips my heel but Maxine, still trapped in her own circle of need, doesn't notice me.

The door to 316 opens and Maxine steps in and drops her purse, peels off her blouse and bra. Slides the skirt down, slips off her underwear and then walks into the bathroom and closes the door.

I pick up her things. Hear water running.

Sitting on the bed, I wait. It is a long wait. I run the story backwards from the dressing room to the bar and the smell of semen and sweat like the worst nightmare of a man in a thyroid dream and then the door opens.

Maxine wears the white terry cloth robe. She's barefoot. Her hair, wet, strings down over the robe. She kneels on the floor in front of me and she says,

Berle, listen to me. I have to talk to her again.

Won't do you any good.

I can still talk some sense into her.

She's made up her mind.

You don't know.

The scars are too thick.

You only see the worst in people, Berle.

Everybody has a rough go at some time, Maxine. Some people give up. Your sister's given up. She likes it where she is.

I can make it up to her.

She's twenty-eight. If she wanted out, she'd be out.

I don't know why I like you you're so hateful.

Not hateful, truthful. You have to see it the way it is.

And how is it, Berle?

There's no way you can save her.

I have to try.

I reach for her to pull her up but she draws back, her eyes as hard as I've ever seen them and when I touch her arm, she leaps up and attacks me squealing and it's a sound I've heard in slaughter pens when the pigs are snared, just before they're strung up by their tendons, just before the throat cuts, just before the river of blood squirts from the gash in the neck. Maxine pounds on me, flailing as she screams but I take it. I don't like it, but I take the blows, the scratches as she unwinds the coil of pain and when she's spent, when the squealing dies down to a whimper, I pull her close, smell her clean scent. As I hold her, I think of Emily on the pole in her leopard skin bikini. I remember the smell of men oozing rut as they eat her with their eyes and I don't tell Maxine that her sister likes that power. She likes knowing men want her and will tuck money in her bikini. She likes it. That's why she'll never give it up.

As I hold Maxine, I know I've got the good sister, flawed and cracked and fragmented, sure, but the one who can be redeemed because down in the dark silence, she is still pure. Through the hurt and the deception, she believes she can save the fallen sister—at least pull her out of the last ring of hell and feed her and clothe her and mother her, but I know it's too late. I've seen it in the eyes, in the wrinkles, in the sag of the skin. Maxine lives in the sky, her feet off the ground, but Emily is earth-bound and the cavern swallowing her has no limit and she'll wander there until one night they find her face down in the mud and when they turn her over, they'll find her sliced from jaw to knee.

Maxine falls quiet then and I hold her. Squeeze her and keep protecting her until she settles into me, fitting against me and for a long time we are fixed together and I feel her breath even out and she relaxes. She whispers,

What would I do without you, Berle?

I want to laugh. I need her more than she needs me. I need the warmth of her skin. I need the fire of her pain to make me feel alive. Every day I need to find her again because only when I find her do I see what I was before—a dead man on a treadmill. I can't go back to that. Not now.

I kiss the face, stroke the damp hair. That's all I need, all I want. Maxine stretches out on the bed and opens the white robe and she looks at me and her mouth is an open invitation and she slowly raises her knees, slowly, ever so slowly raises her knees.

No Signs of Sin

In her sleeping face there are no signs of sin. I can watch her in the dim light forever as the shadows erase the anger lines around her eyes, as the relaxed skin lets go of worry and in those minutes I see not only what she is, but what could have been. In the wrinkles of the forehead there is still the hint of pain pointing to the ravishing of her body by the man who turned her into a whore, the man who bought her, used her, turned her dark.

But as I lie beside her, all of that washes away leaving the problem of what to do next. It would be nice just to stay put here in the hotel, not have to eat, drink, not have to walk out of here. There's comfort in a small prison and I feel like I can stay there for a long time, but I know it has to end in anger and blood.

She stirs.

Her arm flings out, the fingers gripping as if she's holding a hot stone, and then she rolls onto her side, away from me. I touch her bare hip.

I check the time. Three-thirty A.M.

I slide off the bed, head to the bathroom, close the door before turning on the light. I stare at my face in the mirror. My skin is yellow, wrinkled as if I've absorbed all her worry and hurt. She's somehow transferred it to my skin that now sags under the weight. Somewhere in one of those wrinkles there's a dead man and a dead woman and little girl abandoned in a bus station and a stripper in a leopard skin bikini. Running my fingers over the creases, I try to decode which one it is. I splash cold water on my face. Look again at the face unshaven, now two days and three love making sessions old. You'll have to shave, she said, before you do that to me again. I'm all raw. But I like it so don't stop.

Peeling off the plastic from the pack of drug store disposable razors, I select a yellow handled one. I lather my face and carve swathes through the white sea of bubbles baring the skin, now turning smooth, those small highways that go nowhere but from cheek to Adam's apple. I rinse away the suds, watch the short-trimmed hair disappear down the drain—still wondering if I'm cleaning out the pain she felt the first time he sold her on her back to a roughneck oil rig worker from the fields of Wyoming in that trailer.

Studying my face in the mirror...

What am I?

What am I doing?

Why am I doing it?

And then the door opens and Maxine stands in the art deco frame as if she is why the door exists, as if she is why the architect drew the lines the way he did—for me to see her naked, in the light. Naked and unashamed. True. As if in two days she's come to know me well enough to bare her flaws, all the little flaws women have that they think matter but don't. I can tell her I like the belly, like the thighs with just a touch of marbling in them, like the way her breasts sacrifice the tightness of youth to gravity making her so human it aches. She says,

I woke up and you were gone. I thought you were gone for good. It scared me.

I'm right here, I say.

She closes against me, her belly to my back. I look at her face in the mirror, see the faint purple sacs under her eyes now clear of makeup that hides the real her. I see her fingers laced across my belly, the freckled skin reddish against the darkness of my own skin. I say,

I was watching you sleep.

I had a bad dream.

Tell me.

I rinse off the plastic razor, lay it on the sideboard, wipe away the residue of soap.

I can't remember it, she says. I had to wake up to make it go away.

A nightmare?

Not quite. Look at me, I'm a mess.

You're not a mess.

I hate my belly, she says.

I love your belly.

I hate my ass.

I love your ass.

I hate my hair.

You are pretty ragged, I say. That happens when you sweat while you're asleep.

I don't sweat, she says.

I love your sweat.

What do you want, Berle Kubiak?

What do you mean?

You're throwing that word around like confetti.

What word?

Love, she says.

She squeezes me tight, lays her head against my back. I feel her heat, the press of her thighs rubbing mine. Somehow the pain and anguish have fused us together. Some kind of emotional glue, sticky and wet and clingy so clingy I know that if I move, she'll have to glide with me and I like it and I can't help it and she knows it. She says,

You're the only man who makes me want to do that.

Have bad dreams? I say.

Squeeze you hard. There's something about a squeeze that says you mean it.

Do you mean it, Maxine?

I really mean it, she says.

She lets go and turns around and leans against the sink facing me. She raises her hands to my face and strokes the skin with the pads of her fingertips. She studies my eyes. I pull her hand away. She tenses. Hesitates.

I'm afraid now, Berle.

Of what?

You know. Emily. Maybe you're right.

We have to leave the hotel sometime, I say.

We can stay here as long as we want. We can live here.

You know we can't.

She pulls a long white towel off the rack beside the sink and wraps it around her in the way women do leaving just the mounds of her breasts visible. She tucks the end between her breasts and tousles her hair. Small bursts of sparks leap out frizzing her hair. She says,

Look at that.

The electric Maxine. Strands of hair stand straight up like she's wearing a fright wig.

What do you want, Maxine? I say.

I keep putting off what I have to do.

You can't buy her. You can't pull her out of the hole she's in.

Why do you have to be so negative?

I'm being practical.

You're so into detail, you can't see the whole thing.

You're right. I don't know but I've seen women like your sister and they're lost and they're all looking for something they'll never find but they'll keep on looking until...

She deserves a chance.

What are you doing to do? Kidnap her?

Don't be stupid.

We'll talk to her later.

If you're such a mind reader tell me what I'm thinking right now.

Maxine looks at me, pouty lips, wet eyes.

I have no idea what you're thinking.

You're a coward.

I see what I see.

She adjusts the towel then, on tip toes, kisses my cheek. She says,

I'm going back to bed.

I watch the bare calves flex as she tiptoes out of the bathroom. Why did she wrap up in the towel? Why do women tiptoe when they're naked or wet?

Alone, I look at myself again, rub my cheek where I still feel the touch of her lips. The skin is smooth now, slick. It is nice skin. I turn off the light then go back to bed. Maxine lies on top of the sheets, her arms stretched out. The towel is under her, but now open over her belly. She whispers,

Tie me up and fuck me, Berle.

I feel the flushing of my skin, hot burning flush of the blood rush to my face. She lifts her hips, but I don't go for it. Instead of pulling the towel away, I fold it back over her nakedness covering her and she looks puzzled but then, still watching my eyes, she lowers her arms and tucks the towel between her breasts. She says,

I see.

Watching Her

She stands in front of the mirror touching her lips, her cheeks, tugging at an eyelid as if she's looking for some truth hidden in the folds. She doesn't waste time, but with the hand of a painter, traces her lips with red, and then dabs at the lipstick with the tip of a finger. I watch her. She has no idea how beautiful she is standing there, her reflection making two of her, four hands, two mouths. And then she catches me as I stare and she picks up a comb, rakes at her hair that is already perfect—icing on an éclair—and she smiles. I say,

You have to stop primping sometime.

I don't want to leave, she says.

She tucks the comb, the lipstick, the small glass container of perfume into the sack purse—so big an entire family of ravens could nest there—and with a final twirl, she faces me.

Finished, she says.

From the bed, I watch her, dreading what comes next. Dreading the opening of the door to take the first step on the long journey. I say,

I called her while you were in the shower.

How did she sound?

Worried. Come here.

You're the one pushing me to hurry, she says.

Take a minute, I say. Let's make sure.

Instead of sitting, she stands at the foot of the bed, smooths her skirt, messes with the opening of her blouse then, puckish, smiles at me.

You just want to watch, she says.

Yeah. I like watching you.

I get off the bed. She backs up. I reach for her. She pushes me away.

No time for that, she says.

Looking back at the room, I see the art deco dresser and the curved wood and glass mirror over the bed and the drapes of light blue velveteen. I don't want to go. It's been okay, this little vacation in the hollow of nowhere, pulled out of the river of time for three days and two nights. Maxine says,

Now you're the one killing time.

I close the door, carrying the box with the hundreds in it. I follow Maxine to the elevator, take it to the ground floor where the desk clerk waits behind his art deco desk, his eyes still dark ringed and red splotched, his hair now combed slick like the coat of a wet muskrat. He smiles. The diamond in his front tooth is brilliant. He says,

Everything all right, Mr. Kubiak?

I hand him the key and then follow Maxine out into the Portland mist, into crushed summertime fine as powder. As we walk to the BMW, the mist bedews Maxine's hair, sparkles against the fire red hair. She is a mystical priestess rising out of time. She turns to me, waiting. I unlock the door, she slides in. She sits, mist lighting her hair. She says,

I'll never be ready for this.

It'll be over in a sec, I say.

We drive through the rain, the wipers tick ticking across the windshield. Maxine is quiet. Knees drawn together, hands on top of the sack purse. Prim. Proper. She says,

You have the box?

In the trunk.

She lets go of the purse. Pats my hand. She says,

You think of everything detail man.

Kids Playing with Hoses

Emily is a domestic slave like Margaret McDunough. The ultimate step-child.

How could you do that to me? Emily says.

Maxine's facial expression tells me to turn away. The cracks in her skin are a mirror breaking and her lips tremble and instead of leaving her, I touch her. She looks at Emily seated on the footstool, knees together, hands clasped, eyes straight ahead. Maxine whispers,

What was I supposed to do, Emmy?

Emily stands, her jeans tight as wet leather, her red blouse aflare, her black hair hanging down to her shoulders. She says,

Everything after that day was shit, sister. You'll never know what I went through.

I see the searching in Emily's eyes, the slope of her shoulder, and over her shoulder through the window of the trailer, kids playing with a hose. Laughing. Skidding on wet grass. The hose, whipping loose, spews a fountain until one of the kids grabs it and pops the flowing end in his mouth and water squirts out in a spray. I remember Maxine's story about leaving Emily in the Greyhound bus depot alone in the restroom, still holding her blood-stained white dress, naked except for the pair of white panties with the stain down the front. Maxine says,

I couldn't keep you.

Emily, sharp, eyes hot, says,

The police took me, Maxine. But I didn't tell them a thing. Nothing.

What would you have told them?

I saw you kill Ted but I didn't tell them. I know you killed Mama and I protected you and I kept waiting for you to come back but you didn't.

Maybe we ought to go get a cup of coffee, I say.

But both women glare at me as if I'm a foreigner in this country of lost women. I close my mouth and cross my arms. Emily says,

Carl's coming back and I want you gone before he gets here.

Emily walks to the coat rack on the wall of the trailer and pulls out a pack of Slims and shakes one loose and lights it with a gold lighter. Her hands look like Maxine's hands, the way she holds the lighter is the same, snapping it closed, then palming it while she takes the cigarette between middle and index finger. Maxine says,

That's my brand too.

If I'd known that I'd've thrown them away.

What can I do to make it up to you, love?

How do you make up twenty years, Maxine? and not a word. Did you even look?

You think I had it easy? Tell her, Berle, just tell her.

You tell me. Just tell me why you ran out on me. Jesus Christ.

I'm in the middle but it's a comfortable place to be because I see what needs to be and I see that I can do it and so I open up the can of worms and rescue Maxine and I say,

Your sister had a baby, Emily. She lived on the street, she lived in a commune, she's a prisoner in a gilt cage and she didn't have a way to find you until now.

It wasn't easy, Maxine says, finding you. Maybe you could see it my way. Maybe you could have looked for me, you know.

I was eight years old.

Did they treat you right?

No one treated me right until I found Carl, Emily says. Would I be stripping and showing men my pussy if they'd treated me right? First the house in Eugene. I ran when I was ten because I kept having a nightmare about the trailer burning up and you were in it, Maxine. And that made it worse.

I'm sorry, Maxine says. I'm so sorry.

They hunted me down after two days and they stuck me in a place in Oregon City and it was a rat hole but I got out when I was twelve and I never went back.

Emily ducks the Slim into an ashtray on the fold out table beside the front door. She looks at Maxine but instead of the hard glare, there's a touch of humor in her eyes. She says,

But that's not your fault, is it Maxine? If Mama had been good, none of this would have happened.

But she wasn't. I'd never have hurt you, you know that. Come here.

No, Emily says. Carl will be here any minute.

Come with me, Maxine says. I'll take care of you.

I can take care of myself.

You don't have to live here, Maxine says.

What's wrong with here?

Do you own it?

I don't own anything except my spangles and the clothes in my closet and that beat up Honda.

We can take care of you, Maxine says. I need you, baby. I really need you.

I don't want you and I'm sorry you found me because I think it'd have been better to wonder about you because now that I see you, I think I hate you.

We can make it better, baby.

I'm not your baby. I don't want to be anyone's baby.

Maxine draws back like she's been slapped. The tears are there, leaking out of her eyes and she says,

Give me a chance.

Outside I hear the crunch of tires on gravel and the kids playing with the hose scream and the boy holding the hose sprays the windshield of the black Camaro as the car stops in front of the trailer and Carl, the bouncer from the club gets out and chases the boy with the hose and grabs him and tosses him over his shoulder and the three other kids attack and he pulls them all to the ground and he holds them down in a pile and then they are all sitting together and he takes coins from his pocket and each of the kids plucks a coin from his hand. The kids run away and Carl stands, turns off the hose and shakes himself like a dog.

Emily turns to Maxine. She says,

I don't need you, Maxine.

Maxine stands. She takes Emily's hands and she kisses them and then she locks arms with me and she sighs and she says,

I guess we should go, Berle.

Cutting Ties

You don't like to let go of things you've held close all your life. Like Maxine's dream she can save her little sister.

But then reality rushes in and smacks you in the mouth and through the blood and spit you see the logic of the hammer.

You have to let go.

Letting go is hard enough but watching the hooks rip loose from someone's dream is like pulling your guts out through your nose. You share the pain, but there's nothing you can do, especially with a woman like Maxine.

She folds her arms across her chest and in that second of surrender she's no longer young, no longer pure, but she carries her years like a meat jacket weighing her down. The sister, Emily, doesn't cry or beg for help and Maxine closes the book on twenty years of searching. Emily didn't say it's time for you to go. But her body language, the way her back was bent, said get-the-hell-out-of my life.

Maxine takes a deep breath and, clutching the sack purse that's held everything from a hundred grand to tubes of lipstick, she heads for the door. She doesn't look back as she streaks for the BMW. I follow.

She's in place when I settle beside her. I expect tears and blubbering, but she's hard and cold and pulled back down inside herself so deep nothing leaks out. Nothing.

I wait.

Through the grit of the windshield of the BMW, I look at the trailer and I wonder if Maxine sees the same things I see—the little aluminum jail her sister calls home, the grungy never-cleaned windows, the wooden box where the steps used to be. Maxine lays her left hand on my leg but her hand has lost its heat and I remember the warmth the first time she touched me. There's a lot of highway between that first touch and this gesture of surrender. I can feel her thoughts through her fingers and she's saying no to everything. She digs into my thigh, I glance at her, but she's staring straight ahead, her claws hunting for blood. Then, in a voice I've never heard, echoing as if she's living in ice, she says,

I was ready to give her everything. All my life I thought it would be better when I found her, but she won't let me in. What's wrong with me?

You did what a good sister had to do.

I start the BMW, back out of the lot, head for the highway. Maxine says,

You didn't say much in there.

Not my place, not my sister.

What would you have done?

Let go and not look back.

What does that mean?

Did you really think she'd come with you?

I wanted her to.

Let her go and start over.

Are you going to let me go? She asks.

She pulls her hand from my thigh. It's a threat, a question, a promise, but nothing now can cut the ties holding me to her. Maybe a little blood, maybe a little pain, but I'm welded to her like a hunk of steel welded to the side of a ship. She knows it. She still tests me. She says,

I've never given myself to anyone except you. When I was little, I dreamed about someone like you coming to save me because I needed saving. But no one did. I'm not a good person. I know that, but I didn't make my own luck. Men did things to me I didn't ask for. They hurt Emily and I couldn't save her. So how can anyone care about me enough to save me? Even Charlie. I don't see why he wants me because I'm not worth saving but I know I'm worth more than six hundred dollars, don't you think? You can tell me the truth because it won't change anything with us—just tell me what you think I'm worth. If you saw me in that trailer, what would you have paid for me? When I was in that trailer—how can she live in a trailer after what happened to us? I never knew where I was—Utah? Wyoming? Nevada? Men came in and Ted took their money and told me to be nice to them and you know what being nice meant. I don't know how much they paid him, but I know I'm worth more than six hundred dollars so why don't you say something? I'm talking and I can't stop and you can stop me if you just say something because I can't shut up you fucking idiot say something because I can't stop until you tell me what I'm worth but you're not even listening you son of a bitch I hate you you're just like every other man who ever came into that trailer and used me like a toilet because that's what I am, a god damned toilet with a cunt so say something god damn you, just say something.

I pull to the side of the road and shut down the BMW. Maxine is crying, her mouth trembles and everything she's said hangs like dead meat on hooks between us. I take her hand. Empty and cold like the blood has drained out of her. I wait for words because this is the time I don't want to say the one thing that shouldn't be said. Don't want to fall into a trap I can't get out of. I think, run half a dozen lines up to see which one sends chills down my spine and then I realize they're all dangerous, all alligator teeth, tiger claws—every word is a sword. Maxine says,

You hate me so much you can't even talk to me. I'm a slut and who wants to talk to a slut, right? So I'll get out right here and leave you mr clean son of a bitch to your pretty little world.

Maxine, you ask me a question I can't answer. I tell you this—I know you now, I see you here. This is where we are. For me, your past is a foreign country I'll never get to. The language they speak there isn't one I want to learn. There's a lot I don't know, but I do know that there's nothing you can say that will drive me away. I don't care what you've done but I do know that if I could, I'd go back and resurrect Ted so I could kill him a dozen times for what he did to you. I will never forget what he did to you and what you mother did to you but, Maxine, I'm not putting a value of who you are or what you mean to me. Nothing can change that.

I tried to buy her just like Charlie tried to buy me.

What would your money have bought?

You haven't tried to buy me, she says.

You think I'm worth more than six hundred dollars?

Kids Make Me Want to Vomit

In the twilight, the edges of day fuzz and the fatigue in my back bends me closer to the wheel. Sitting in the BMW makes me realize how the last three days have caught up with me, how tight I am from the neck down like a man whose muscles have hardened into stone.

Maxine sits beside me, chastised, purified, her mind cleansed by the act of leaving Emily in the little trailer but still bound up inside, looking for the escape valve. I glance at her, see the slow slope of her shoulders, the relaxed bend of her leg as she sits with one knee tucked under her. It's as if we've traveled a hundred years together, lived a full rich life as a couple.

I think about speed. Remember the whine of tires on pavement. I find some relief in running fast. Speed blurs the edges of time and I lose myself in that speed.   Who am I? What am I?

In three days, my world has slowed down and for the first time I see it.

Maxine shifts in the seat, untucks her leg and turns to face me. Her skin, taking the blue lights of the dash, blackens. My eyes, hungry for her, rake her like prey, but she isn't, right now, prey. She is an angel cleansed and in her face, I see the calmness of sacrifice. She clears her throat. She says,

I've been thinking.

I wait, but she doesn't go on. The speedometer now reads zero. No white line, no late night highway thick with semi traffic. Zero.

I've been thinking about the one thing we still have to work out.

Okay. What's that?

Probably nothing, but we still have to talk about it.

What do you want to tell me?

She pops the door, slides out. I follow.

To our left there is a grove of trees and just beyond the trees, a river flows, and between the trees and the river, a set of railroad tracks runs north and south. In the dim light of parking lot lamps Maxine stands with her back to me, electric straight, staring ahead. Hooked on her Slims, she doesn't light one, but holds the pack in her hand waiting.

A train hums by, blurred by the trees. As the train passes, the engineer lays on the horn. It is very dark in the grove. I smell the scent of pine and dust. I smell the residue of diesel. In the distance, the night is punctuated with the growl of semis, the whir of cars moving fast, the musical nocturne of trucks wheeling toward Seattle, grinding up the pass to drop over towards Ellensburg and Yakima. Then, there is a rest, a hole in the symphony, a quiet moment. Maxine turns to me and she says,

I don't know what you think about kids.

What about kids?

Do you want kids?

I haven't thought about kids.

Charlie wanted me to have kids. I told him to go to hell.

How did he take that?

He said it was okay but it wasn't. He wanted kids.

Do I need to know this?

No secrets, isn't that the new mantra?

No secrets.

So how do you feel about kids?

You mean do I want to have kids?

I'm too old to have kids, Maxine says.

That settles that.

You're okay with that?

You're too old, I say. That's that.

The idea of having kids makes me want to vomit. That's why I had two abortions.

Maxine, it's tomorrow I'm thinking of.

And what if tomorrow you suddenly find out that you want kids. I'm too old. In a couple of years I'll be like a truck without an engine. I'm thinking what if you decide you need to leave a little Berle in the world, so what do you do with me?

I hear the music of the nighttime highway—the whine of rubber on concrete, the counterpoint of gears downshifting to the staccato of jake brakes tugging at the speeding of semis slipping on their way to dawn. I say,

You're worried I'll want a kid.

If you want kids, you'll have to look somewhere else.

Where are you going with this now, Maxine?

So you don't want to leave a little you?

No.

What do you want? She says. What if after we see Charlie all the juice is sapped from your engine?

My engine?

From us, she says. All the juice goes away and you don't want me anymore.

Is that all you think I am? A guy who's out for the juice of...this?

You had your women in Reno. It's exciting, isn't it? Sleeping with another man's woman, wondering if he's onto you, wondering if he's just outside the door waiting with a gun in his hand?

You bring that up. Why?

You don't get a charge out of that?

So this isn't about kids.

I need to know, Berle. When you look at me, what do you see? Do you see a dried up hag? A slut? A whore who's fucked hundreds of men? What do you see?

There it is. The tiger trap, the man trap, the one thing that can maim me, the one thing I shouldn't say because there's no answer. So I do what I have done before. I pull her to me, feel her resist then relax. I run my hands over her back, press her against me. Thinking. I say,

I don't like those words. Hag. Slut. Whore. That's not you. You hear me? I'll tell you. When I look at you, I see a woman I want to be with. No conditions. Two rules—wake up in the same bed every morning, never go to bed mad. That's what I want.

She looks up at me. In the faint light, her eyes glitter like a cat's. She takes a deep breath, then she says,

You're such a rotten liar.

*****

Clyde stands at the front desk and he pulls off his thick lenses and he wipes at them with a red bandana. The grease smears shiny as foil. Glasses back on, he looks at the Asian night clerk, looks at the half shaved head, the half Mohawk giving her an asymmetry that makes her look like the two halves of two people joined with glue at a seam in her skull and he says,

She's a tall red-head about 35, may be with a guy.

The clerk looks at Clyde and she says,

Let me see a badge.

What?

A badge. You a cop?

Clyde wants to throttle her but he holds back, looks at the lids deep stained with eye shadow. He says,

Look, just help me out here.

Nobody like that staying here, the clerk says.

Clean Underwear, Clean Socks

She's quiet, the darkness in her molten. Arms folded, she leans against the door as I cruise back downtown to the

Franklin Hotel where I park, shut down the 850 and wait. Maxine doesn't budge.

I open the door, slide out.

I'm tired, she says.

I go around the car to her, hold her for a moment tight, now warm. She's softness, molded into my side. I circle her waist, hand on her belly as we walk into the hotel.

The lobby of the Franklin is lit with art deco gold table lamps that shine on black marble tops. The night clerk is a tall thin rangy Asian woman wearing oversized glasses on a silver chain. Her hair cut in an asymmetrical half-shaved Mohawk. She wears dangly earrings that chime when she moves her head.

Any messages for Kubiak?

Uh huh.

Calls?

Nope.

The night clerk smiles. I see her front teeth are filed and there is a bright spot in her left incisor. It's a diamond. I say,

Does that hurt? The tooth?

No more than a tattoo, she says. Or a piercing.

You're pierced? I say.

She looks at me over the rims of the glasses, her mouth pursed in a mocking and cynical sneer, then with a glance at Maxine, she says,

Are you curious or just taking a survey?

A little curious.

You should try it, she says.

The piercing or the tattoo?

Hand and glove, Mr. Kubiak.

Maxine tugs on my arm and we walk hip to hip to the elevator to the room where she kicks off her high heels. She says,

Something about this place.

You mean the night clerk?

And the day clerk.

World's changing every day, I say.

She's going to hate me.

I'm going to shower, I say.

You'll need clean underwear, she says. Won't you?

I go to the phone, call the desk, tell the woman with the diamond in her tooth that I need some underwear and socks. Size 34 waist, any color, any color on the socks.

Black, Maxine shouts, get black BVDs. They're so cute.

Black, I say to the desk clerk, but any color will do if you can't find black.

It's kind of late, the night clerk says.

I saw an all-night drugstore down the street, I say. They'll have something.

It'll be a while, she says.

I'm in for the night, I say. About the piercing...

Yeah.

Does it hurt?

Big tattoo, she says, lots of blood.

A big one?

Big enough, she says. It's a tramp stamp. A big eagle in the small of my back. So guys have something to look at. It's red and black and yellow. Hurt like a son of a bitch.

Hanging up, I turn to Maxine who's stretched out on the bed on her belly, feet in the air, smoking a Slim. She says,

Thank you for everything.

Can I take my shower now?

Can I watch?

*****

The shower is hot. I soap up with hotel shampoo. Brush my teeth with the hotel brush and comb my hair with the hotel comb and looking in the mirror I see a crazy man on the lam with a woman he doesn't know going somewhere he doesn't understand and there's a half million dollars in the bedroom suite and there's a woman on the bed waiting for who knows what and I figure I've got my mojo working but I've lost my job, lost my house, run off with the boss's woman and I guess it's just crazy enough to be interesting if I'm not dead in the morning.

Donning the second white robe, I fold my sweaty shirt and pants, stinky socks and shorts into a stack and go back out to Maxine.

She's on the bed, on her side wearing nothing but green underwear. Her hair's spread out on the pillow like a red water fall. I pull up a chair. I want to look at her while she's not in motion. She's a lot like the 850—even standing still she's a blur, looks like she's breaking the sound barrier. I lean down, look at her feet with the painted emerald toenails, look at the ankles, small, look at the calves, smooth. And the freckles like candy sprinkles on an ice cream cone, look at her face now soft and relaxed, glowing. Her mouth is open so the lips arch into a small bow, cracked, a little bit dry, a tiny crack crusted under the lipstick that's still bright red. Her right hand buried under the red hair, lays palm down so I see her hand and fingers and the small chip in her middle fingernail that lets the pink show through. That's how she is—all fluff and emeralds on the outside but pink and clean and pure on the inside.

There's a rap on the door. I answer. The bell boy, dressed in his black and white uniform, looks like a normal middle-American. Short cut hair, no tattoos, no nose piercings, no diamond teeth, no painted fingernails. He could be a football player or a teller in a bank. There's a wide grin on his face. He says,

Mr. Kubiak, I found the items you need. It comes to thirty-one fifty.

He hands me a sack with the name of a drugstore on it. I turn back to the room, to the stacks of hundred-dollar bills in the box by the bed and I pull out a bill and go back and hand it to him and he says,

Whoa, that's way too much for shorts and socks.

Take it, I say. It's late, you did good.

Jeez, sir, wow.

Split it with the night clerk.

Nuunuu, he says. Her name is Nuunuu.

Split it with Nuunuu then.

He bows and backs away and I watch him skip down the corridor to the elevator and when the bell dings, I turn to the room to see Maxine's eyes open and she's smiling and she says,

Come here. Now that you're clean and sweet I want a bite.

I sit on the bed, toss the sack with the shorts and socks on the chair. I say.

What now, Maxine?

You gotta be kidding me, she says.

Maybe we don't do the obvious.

Oh, she says. Sex is easy, friendship is hard? Is that it?

What we have isn't friendship, I say.

What is it then?

She sits up. She looks at me, minxy eyes, pouty lips, flared nostrils. She says,

Don't tell me you just want to talk?

Yeah, I say. We need to talk about Charlie and that money and your sister.

Am I too old for you, Berle? You don't like older women?

I'm here. That's not what I want to talk about.

Then what?

She slides a hand over mine. I look down at the chipped fingernail, the smooth freckled skin. For the first time I notice that she wears her wristwatch on her right hand. I've never seen that wristwatch before. I touch it, then look at her. I say,

You have to know some things about me.

I already know everything I need to know.

When I was twelve, I say, I went boating with my mom and dad on Lake Wallula…

Smashed by a Tornado

You're 32, Berle and you still call them Mom and Dad?

You have to listen, Maxine. I've never talked about this and I don't know if I can say it without breaking up.

She touches me then. Her hand cool and soft and I sit on the edge of the bed looking at the black face of the TV against the far wall and in it I see us reflected—white robe, green underwear, the headboard a backdrop like a proscenium arch. I say,

It was July and hot. It's always hot on the lake in July. We were out about halfway. You could see the Gap at the far end of the lake. My mother was setting out lunch on deck. She told me to go swimming before we ate. My father was below tinkering with the engine because he always tinkered with it—he had a knack for engines. So I dove in and swam a hundred yards because I'm a good swimmer. Then I look back and it was like a movie. My eyes are at water level but I can see my mother on deck and aimed right at the boat, I see a Tornado cutting toward her. I shouted but I'm in the water and my mother looks out at me just as the Tornado slams into her, taking the boat amidships and the boat explodes. The Tornado flips over the deck and comes down keel up and two bodies parachute into the water. I swim back to our boat, but she's already on fire and I don't see my mother and she's breaking up and before I can get back to her, she goes down and all that's left is the fire.

I look up from the blank TV, look at Maxine and she's staring at me, unblinking. I see something in her eyes as she searches my face. I say,

This is harder than I thought it would be.

What happened to them?

They were both dead. The guys in the Tornado weren't hurt but my mom and dad both burned to death and there was nothing anyone could do.

I'm sorry, Maxine says.

I thought you'd know all this already.

He didn't go that deep, she says.

Just checked my medical history, I say. Checked me out for STDs and criminal past.

She laughs, a tittering giggle and she squeezes my hand until it hurts and she says,

I'm sorry. I didn't mean to laugh, but you make me laugh when you get all cynical on me. And no, he didn't check for STDs.

Why not? I say. It's the Twenty-first century. Half of everybody either has herpes or is living with someone who does.

There you go again, Maxine says. I need to know the rest. You're twelve when this happens. Then what? You don't leave a twelve-year-old boy alone.

Yeah, I say. Twelve. The same age you were when your mother died. So that makes us a lot alike.

She stops for a second, her hand relaxes. Her fingers, cool, the nails retracted.

You want to hear the rest?

I need to hear the rest, she says.

The river police arrested the two guys on the Tornado. There was a trial. They went to jail for negligent homicide because they were drunk. I went into a foster home.

No other family? She asks.

No other family. My mother's folks were dead by the time I was six. My dad was an only child, no brothers, sisters, aunts or anything and his folks died early too. I had the settlement money in trust.

The settlement?

The insurance on the two drunks paid a lump sum into a trust my dad had already set up for me. His lawyer ran it until I was eighteen.

And that's how you bought your house?

Nope. That's the ancestral home. My dad built it and with the insurance for him and my mother—which was a lot of money because they took care of one another—I could've lived the rest of my life and never lifted a finger.

But you stayed in the Valley? Why?

I don't know. I went to Eastern. Didn't want to go too far.

I'm glad you decided not to leave, she says.

I roll onto the bed beside her. She looks calm and clear. I'm glad how she handles it. Instead of getting all weepy and sentimental, she's a rock. I try to imagine her at twelve in the bed of the man who bought her, but I can't get hold of her pain and I ask myself then if I've made a mistake telling her all that because she doesn't need that load, but she has to see me for what I am. I wonder if she sees the deep cracks.

Were they good to you?

Who?

Your foster parents.

The Kubiaks. Yeah. They wanted to adopt me, but that didn't happen so I just took their name instead.

So you're not a real Kubiak?

Nope. Half mutt, half mongrel. The pure-bred All-American bloodline.

Are they still alive?

I never see them, but yeah. When I got my degree, I gave them a quarter of a million dollars so they could go be amateur archeologists in Peru. They're on a dig somewhere in the desert right now.

Do you have something to ask me? She says.

I don't need to ask you anything except what do we do now?

What do you want to do now?

I touch her arm, rub her skin with its map of freckles. With the tip of my finger, I trace the freckles. She says,

What are you doing?

Writing your story, I say. It's in the dots on your body. All of it. If I do it right, it's like reading an ancient scroll in a forgotten language.

Maxine presses her hand over mine. She studies the two hands together—mine big and wide, the nails broad and clipped, hers slender and freckled with that single chip in the nail.

It's a story in two parts, she says. Before Berle and after Berle.

And Charlie? Where does he fit in?

Charlie—ancient history, she says.

And she looks at me and gets up and kneels on the bed. She takes my hands and presses them together. She says,

The story gets more interesting the deeper you get into it.

Pulling me down, she kisses me and it is a long, slow, intense kiss that I don't want to end.

But There was More

She lies on her right side facing me, small beads of sweat clotting her forehead, her hair spread out on the pillow with the precision of a painter posing her. She rests her left hand on my chest and she says,

Does it bother you being in bed with someone named Max?

If Max has your equipment it's a machine I can operate.

You are a heavy equipment operator, she says, that's for sure.

Yeah, working with my hands, I can get into my work.

I know.

She sits up, leans against the headboard, unashamed now. The white sheet runs like a river over her thighs. She says,

Is there anything you want to ask me?

Is there anything you want to tell me?

I don't know where to start.

I look at her propped against the brown wood. She's got a frown on her face. She says,

Don't look at me like that, please.

How am I looking at you?

The magic eye. It's like you're looking through me.

Okay, I say. I have a question.

That's better.

You didn't learn how to do that reading a book, did you?

You want me to be ashamed of my skills? I've got plenty to be ashamed of, but that's not one of them.

No, I'm not trying to shame you. I like it. I like it a lot. But what does that mean? Plenty to be ashamed of?

You mean besides the fact that I killed my mother and the man she sold me to?

You were just a kid. Kids are like puppy dogs— they're not ashamed of what they do.

There are some things I can't talk about right now.

Because why?

Because, she says, I don't want to wreck this moment, right here, with stuff that might make you hate me.

I sit up, cross legged on the bed, facing her, my own shame now a tired puppy nestled between my legs. She glances at me and she smiles and then she crawls to me and lays her head in my lap and the weight of her feels good, feels comfortable. She talks facing away as if talking to the wall makes it easier. She tells me about meeting Charlie when she was waitressing at the Hill Top Café in Grants Pass and how he passed through Oregon once a week on his sales route from Redding to Vancouver and how he hustled her and asked her to marry him.

But you didn't you marry him.

She's quiet for a long time, fidgety. I feel her hands flex in mine like mice caught in a cage, afraid to move. I see her censoring the story, measuring the details she wants to serve up while cutting out the sordid parts until, at last, she says,

What the hell. None of it matters now, does it? Does it?

She turns to face me. I let go of her hands. She pulls away. Body erect. Her freckles glistening with sweat and light. She says,

All right. I started sleeping with him, but I told him I'd never marry him. He wanted it and the more I resisted, the harder he tried but Charlie's a cocksman, Berle. He's got kids strung all up and down the coast. I'm not sure how many, but at least eight and he supports them—most of them anyway. Some of the women don't want to take his shit, but he sends birthday cards and Christmas presents.

Is that what you're ashamed of? I say. That you slept with him for money?

I didn't say...you're right. I did. For money. For a year but that's not what I meant.

You told me the story has two parts, Max. Before Berle and After Berle. Well, my story has two parts and nothing that happened before we got in that car matters to me. This is what matters.

She looks away. Closes her eyes. She's churning the facts again, working the story she wants to tell me. I say,

Don't fudge it, Maxine. You have to tell it all.

I worked part time in that fucking café, she says. A woman can't make it on tips. I got sick of guys hitting on me, patting my ass, smiling at them so they'd drop a buck on the table.

That's when Charlie came along?

I had a history, you know. My mother was a whore, so fucking for money is almost second nature to me. Even though I knew Charlie had a string of kids—he told me that when we had this kind of a talk one night when he stayed over—I went with him because he'd already started his business in Yakima and he came up to Grants Pass just to see me and I told him that night I'd live with him but I'd never marry him and I wouldn't produce any bastard kids for him and he said that was all right, all he wanted was for me to be with him. For ten years I fucked him for money.

Four hundred and fifty thousand is a lot of money, I say. If you marry him, it's half yours in this state.

Now it's all mine, isn't it?

Not if he sics the law on you.

It won't be the law he sics on me.

Four hundred and fifty thousand dollars? Why won't he?

It's dark money, she says. He uses it for pay offs. He uses it for his kids. He uses it to buy dark things I don't want to talk about.

Twice you said dark, Maxine.

And you're not ashamed to sleep with someone named Max?

I slept with someone named Sam, and I slept with a Charlene who liked to be called Charlie. A name doesn't change anything. Tell me the rest.

I moved to Yakima. For the money. I'm worth every penny.

You didn't want kids.

He wanted more kids, but I laid down the law. I fuck him for money, but there're no kids. Ever.

Then what did you want from him?

She lets her eyes search my face. Then silence. I wait. No hurry. I know it will all come out when she's ready to let it out. Then she says,

We never spend enough time just looking at eyes, you know. We hate the eyes because of what they've seen. If I'd spent time looking at Charlie's eyes, I'd have seen his darkness.

What do you see in my face? I say.

Your eyes are deep but they're pure. You don't have my darkness in you and that's why I'm worried about you.

You're worried about me.

Charlie's not human, Berle.

He's a man.

That's the problem. You didn't look deep enough. On the surface he does human things but when the time comes, he turns.

What're you telling me, Max?

Max. You like the name, don't you?

I like you, I say. If you're named Axel, I'd still like you.

Enough to die for me?

If that's what happens.

That's what it'll take, she says.

She turns away. Slides off the bed. Facing me, she stretches. The belly shimmers, she reaches up and musses her hair and small electric sparks zap her fingers and she laughs. She says,

Maxine the electric machine.

What are you doing, Maxine?

Do you feel something for me, Berle?

After all we've done you ask that?

Your own damage is pretty deep, isn't it, Hon?

Hon. The first time you're called me anything but Berle.

Just like the old married folk, she says.

Are you proposing to me? I say.

That's exactly what I'm doing, she says.

There's a call on the room phone. I answer. It's the desk clerk telling me that there's a package at the desk. I tell her to bring it up.

The Box with a Head in It

The desk clerk with the chiming earrings and half-Mohawk stands in the door holding a box. She says,

A man said to bring this to you.

What is it? Maxine asks.

She's on the bed, knees pulled up to her chest, arms locked around her knees.

A box, I say.

Is it a shrunken head? Maxine says.

I don't know.

I told you Charlie isn't a normal human being.

I open the box and inside there's a head. A head shrunk like a prune, a bone through the nose, small freckles on the cheeks black as ants. Lips stitched shut, the ears pierced and studded with emeralds. The eyes, closed, small white stitches in the lids, the hair long and blond straggles in the bottom of the box like worms working their way up and over the neck.

I set the box on a chair and step back. Have to take a deep breath. Maxine says,

That son of a bitch. It's Clyde.

This is Clyde.

No, Clyde left it here.

You knew about this?

Is it a blond head with emerald earrings?

I sit on the bed. Maxine rocks back and forth. That head of fiery red hair shimmering with each movement.

What's going on, Maxine.

It's Charlie's way of saying hello.

Who's in the box?

A message, she says.

To me?

To you. To me. But you're dead now.

Charlie did this?

She hums a tune I didn't know. Then, nervous, she gets off the bed, the red hair in the lamp light shining and she strolls to the table, opens her purse, plucks out a fresh pack of Slims, peels the wrapper loose, picks a smoke from the pack and lights it with her gold lighter then she turns to face me.

Am I worth it, Berle? Worth getting your head shrunk?

I'm not dead yet.

Oh, you're dead. You are you're just too fucking dumb to fall down. What are we going to do?

Tell me about the head.

The heads. There are six of them.

Jesus Christ.

Charlie buries the bodies in concrete foundations and shrinks the heads.

I take that deep breath. Head spinning, full of images of dead men in concrete floating through my mind as I look at the box, then at the woman her legs tanned, skin smooth. I say,

Buries them? I poured every yard of concrete that came out of that batch plant and I don't know about that. How can he do that and me not know anything about it?

Clyde, she says.

She sits on the bed, cigarette burning a thin trail of smoke. She is bare foot, toenails painted emerald green. I think about green. Green on a red head always looks good. Especially if the eyes are green.

What about Clyde?

He does it, Maxine says. He does whatever Charlie says.

I feel like an 8.5 quake has just hit, but the rafters don't rattle and the glasses on the sidebar don't shake. I remember guys not showing up for work. Good guys who worked hard but one day just didn't show up on the job.

You're next, Maxine says.

She gets off the bed, goes to the window. Standing in the light in a halo of smoke from the Slim, she looks like an angel descending through the cold breath of god almighty. She giggles. Grinds out the Slim in the ash tray on the deck then comes over to me, kneels, lifts my chin with the hook of her red-painted index fingernail and she kisses me.

He uses me as bait, she says. He baits the trap with these...

She cups her breasts in her hands and pushes them up and there is anguish in her eyes, a crinkling at the corners, a tension. Taking a breath, she says,

And then when the suckers bite, he has Clyde wring their necks and bring them to the house where...well...you don't need me to tell you. You'll be there soon enough.

She straightens. Wheels around. My head is spinning now with images of Clyde and Charlie and men with their necks wrung and their heads shrunk.

Are you going to run, Berle? Clyde's probably out there right now waiting. He uses a big club to the knees to take you down then he binds you up with baling wire so your hands go numb and your fingers turn black.

She looks at me. A distant look, like someone watching a friend disappear under water. She says,

And then, when you're just a crawling lump of blackened flesh, Charlie comes at you with the chainsaw.

And you don't say anything to the cops?

Cops? Charlie owns the cops. I tried to leave six times. Six times I ran off and he sics that bloodhound Clyde on my trail and there's never any getting away.

You like that? You like knowing men die because of you?

I don't like it, I don't dislike it, it's what happens. I tried, Berle. I really tried.

But you don't say no when the sucker's in the trap?

She turns her back. I see a damaged woman with blood on her hands. Under the red hair and tanned skin there is a little girl who never grew up, a little girl in a woman's body. She says,

I want to. I thought maybe you were the one.

I like my head where it is.

She walks to the box on the chair. It is a wooden box with brass studs ringing the lid, brass studs down the sides, a small brass hasp on the front with no lock in it. She lifts the lid.

She looks in the box and then turns, arms crossed. She puckers up, trembling. I stand, pull her close, feel the heat of her skin, the soft skin, taste her Slims in her hair.

His name is Chad, she says. He worked for Charlie for a year.

I remember Chad. He didn't show up the day before we poured the foundation on the bank.

I sleep on top of him every night, she says. Charlie thinks it's funny to fuck me on top of a dead man's head in a box under the bed.

She stops shaking.

How does he shrink the heads?

In the basement. He's got a whole mummy lab down there.

Jesus. How come you don't rat him out?

She pulls away. Looks at me. She says,

He knows my dirty little secret.

What secret?

I told you. I killed my mother and the man she sold me to.

You know I don't really believe you.

I know you didn't believe me until Emily blurted it out. I killed them with an ax, Berle. Both of them. Charlie owns me. He can do what he wants with me but he can't get it up unless there's someone in the trap.

And that was me this time?

I let go of her. Back away from her. Look at her face. Looking for the tell, the sign that she is lying to me, but there is that head and it is in a box and I knew the man the head belonged to and the head is shrunken and there are the earrings of the man I used to know.

I'm sorry, she says. Maybe you should run while you have a chance.

She covers her nakedness now, in this minute of unveiling, she covers herself with a green shift she pulls from that thousand ton sack purse—how did she get all that in there?—and she flips her hair and lets out a sigh.

Stupid Simple

She stands there, a red-headed vision, you get to see only once in your life. I feel like she's hit me in the head with a two by four cut from the stupid-tree. Stupid because I didn't think it out past where we are right then. Driven by my gonads, brain numbed by the scent of her body and the curve of her breasts and the memory of those freckles in the sunlight beside the swimming pool, I have gone stupid and I know it. When something happens that you never dreamed of, you're stymied by reality. I never thought I'd be in a hotel room with her naked on a bed. I never thought it would get that deep. I never expected her to be standing there telling me she wanted me to marry her, to live with her, to get old with her.

The future on the other side of the door is blank. Empty. It's nothing. Everything. I take a minute to work it out and I have a choice—to lie or to tell her the truth. It takes me twenty seconds to come up with the right choice because at this point there's no percentage in anything but the truth. I say,

Where does this go, Maxine?

You've been in hotel rooms with women, she said.

I don't care about anything except what's happening right here, right now.

So it's a no?

A no?

You don't want me?

What do you mean?

I'm asking you, Berle Kubiak—what are your intentions?

The green shift is a veil covering her innocence in a robe of green pain. I take a shallow breath. The head in the box. Clyde. My intentions? It's a crossroads—truth or lie. I say,

There's a shrunken head in that box and I might be next and I don't know what's going to knock on that door or when. Charlie's not ever going to let you go.

He'll be glad to get me back. I know too much.

Tell me everything then.

You're a pain in the ass, she says

But she sits down on the edge of the bed and hangs her head and I feel the weight on her. I think about a little girl sleeping in the back of a station wagon, I think about a little girl in a trailer in Wyoming and men taking her and I want to erase all of that. I want to peel off the past leaving only this minute. I say,

What did she do? Your mother.

I told you. It wasn't pretty and they treated her like shit but what choice did she have?

I touch the nape of Maxine's neck, brush her hair aside and rub at the knots at the base of her skull. There are always knots there when you confess, when the pain tears your life out of your body. Maxine says,

He never touched me like that.

She turns to face me and takes my hands and she kisses them and she says.

You're right. You have to know everything or nothing matters because I can't live behind the mask anymore. I guess that's why I tried to leave him but I couldn't because you never leave until you have somewhere to go and you're where I'm going, Berle Kubiak.

How long?

What?

How long did you sleep in the car?

Two years. She'd entertain her clients in the front seat and I'm sleeping in the back and one night one of them gets tired of her and asks about me.

That's when she sold you?

She drew the line that night, Maxine says. But when I was ten she sold me.

When she says the words sold me, her voice quakes and her hands tremble but she doesn't cry. It's as if all the crying died leaving emptiness. A few years ago I wouldn't have known what to do—to talk, to kiss her, to leave her, to lie with her—but now I've had a lesson in life, and the proof is in the box with the head in it. I sit and hold her and don't say anything and when she raises her head, her eyes are red and dry and there isn't a sob anywhere. She says,

Charlie read me so right. He looked at me and he saw every scar, every secret, every wound, all the blood.

What did he do to you?

Are you the one, Berle?

You mean what are my intentions?

What are your intentions?

My intentions are to do what you need me to do and then do it again until you don't need it anymore and then I'll find something else to do for you.

She looks at me and the hurt little girl who hid in the back of a station wagon while her mother serviced men in the front seat is gone and in her place there is this full bodied, full throated, red haired woman with love in her green eyes and love on her wet lips but she can't say it. The words are too big, too hard, too tricky, so tricky or too used up she can't use them. I know them. I look at her eyes and I want to say the words, but I'm the fish whose mouth opens and closes and nothing comes out but she knows what I mean and she squeezes my hands until bone cracks. She clears her throat and she wants to speak. She sighs. The shift loosens and she smiles. The heat of her body has changed. I still smell the scent of her soap, scent of her natural perfume but everything now is deeper and richer and thicker.

In a low, gravelly voice, the voice that means just one thing no matter what the words are, she says,

Be gentle.

And we lie down and this time it is a slow and deliberate exploration and she's not like any woman I've ever had and it's not like anywhere I've ever been. I thought I knew her but every inch of her is now foreign country no hand has ever explored. It is perfect. I know it will get worse but I don't care because I'm stupid and I'm in love and I just don't care.

The head is still in the box but its eyes are stitched shut and they cannot see what we are doing, doing it in a way I have never done it before and in doing it, we become more than pure, we become what we were before we tasted sin. That is what forever feels like.

Clips of Death

It's late when she looks at me and where I used to see empty space behind her eyes when she thought she was nothing but pain and anguish, hurt and fear, she is smooth, she is soft, and we have both lost what we were before. She straddles me and holds my arms out like I'm a criminal crucified and her eyes are nails driving into my brain and then she softens and she relaxes and she says,

What's wrong?

Nothing wrong with me. Now.

You can't lie to me after this.

All right. It's bothering me, I say. Your story. Sometimes you're eight when you mother sells you and sometimes you're twelve. I don't know what to believe.

Does it matter? Christ almighty, Berle, you give me all this shit about details and what matters is that it happened. Grown men were fucking me. That's what happened. Again and again and fucking again. That's what I remember.

She releases me and we flip back to the way it was before and I want to shoot myself for breaking the shell. It's like with a half dozen words I've uncovered her shame and she reaches for the sheet and tugs it up to her chin and her eyes are hard green emeralds sparked with a ray of hate.

I wait for the tears, but she gets off the bed dragging the sheet with her like a bridal train and she disappears into the bathroom and I hear water running and then she comes back pink. She says,

I just washed the taste of men out of my mouth.

You want to start over? I say.

What do I have to do to make you believe me?

You told Charlie what you told me, didn't you?

Everything, well, except maybe I left out a few things. At first he didn't believe me. I hate that. He treats me like a little girl—his money, his business, his car, his house. I'm his little girl until he wants me and then I'm not a little girl. He can't see pain, Berle. If it doesn't turn into money, he doesn't have any use for it. That new crusher and the new hopper? The new conveyor belts? That's all he cares about. With Charlie there are two speeds—money and off. When he's not thinking about money, he's asleep and then he dreams about it.

As she talks, her mouth tightens, her eyes narrow as if she has to squint to keep all the hurt inside her and all I've done is dig at her pain trying to find some meaning in it. I've shattered her with words.

She pulls away from me then and disappears to the bathroom.

*****

MAXINE

I lie awake for two hours watching streetlights play on the ceiling. I think about being stupid and simple and how many times I've said it, the one thing that just pops out of your mouth before you have time to throttle it.

*****

At six o'clock I get up, get dressed, go to the lobby. The desk clerk is the slick creamy skinned boy with his baby face and the black circles under his eyes. He says,

Is everything all right, Mr Kubiak?

Just great, I say. Just great.

I walk out, take my time thinking about what's next and do I have a choice? Does love do that to you? Take away your anchor, set you adrift in a sea worry? I think about returning to Yakima. What happens then? I lose my head?

It takes me an hour to work it all out.

*****

In the room, Maxine is dressed, hair combed and brushed, lipstick, eye liner. She's smoking a Slim when I enter. She says.

Where did you go?

To see a man about a horse.

Why didn't you wake me?

You needed your sleep, I say.

Come on then, she says.

Where to this time? Idaho?

Just come with me, she says. That's all I ask.

I carry the wooden box with the brass brads and the shrunken head. Maxine says,

Leave it.

Don't want to leave it, I say.

*****

We take the elevator down. Silence. Find the 850 on the street—no parking ticket. I leave the box with the head in the trunk. A shrunken head. Soon to be my head. I say,

Where to?

Tacoma Way and 6th.

I punch the address into the GPS and drive in silence to the Portland Herald where she tells the clerk that she needs to check the archives.

The clerk writes out a slip and Maxine leads me into a bank of computers and she pulls up a chair and flips through the screens, brings up a sheet from 21 years ago, scrolls to a headline with a date and a photograph of a young girl and under the photo it says Missing.

Maxine scrolls down the page to the article and I read about a double murder in a trailer park in Oregon City and how the missing girl named Maxine Mallory was last seen leaving the park with an eight year old girl found later at the Greyhound Bus Depot.

Maxine shuts off the archive. Gets up. Faces me. I say,

Why did you leave her?

I wanted to protect her but he'd already ruined her

She draws a Slim from the purse and I say that she can't smoke in the building and we go outside and she lights it and fiddles with it like she's puzzling out the secrets of tobacco.

Back in the 850 we sit there, me thinking about how I'm going to make it up to her for doubting her and what to do about my house and when do I call Charlie to tell him I quit and I've got his woman and we're going to live happily ever after. Maxine glares straight ahead, hands in her lap and all I can do is smell the scent of fresh lipstick and soap and under the soap the faint odor of her sex—all that's left of the night and I can't help it but it makes me hard again and I look at her, a worried look on her face and it's not the face I know, not the face of a woman lying beside a pool on a deck chair soaking up the sun, not the face of a woman confessing that she's killed two people, not the face of a thief with half a million dollars in a box wrapped in brown paper, it's the face of a woman worried and lost and confused and I feel, feel it, deep for the first time—I don't have just a woman, not just any woman, but the woman…I…love…but I have to know. I'm the detail guy and I have to know.

How It Happened

Tell me how it happened.
You don't need to know.
No secrets now, Maxine.
You make me so god damned mad.

Just tell me what happened.

She looks at me and there is the dark wall she throws up when I get too close but I know that the only way to save her is to open up the darkness and to look into it. It's hard for her to let go and so I take her hand and sit facing her and she looks at our hands. She says,

You're the first guy ever to just hold my hands.

There aren't any roadmaps for this trip, Maxine. We have to find our own way. You'll hate me when you see how terrible I am.

Just tell me how it happened.

Her face is flushed as if she's looking back in time to the night, a long time ago, she says,

I was with Ted watching TV and there was a knock on the door. He opened it and...I can't go on.

Just a little step at a time, I say.

She clutches my hands like they're anchors holding her down. She says,

It was my mother and she had Emily and she said here she is. Ted shoved me off the sofa and made Emily sit down with him and he rubbed her arms and he said, you are a little darling, aren't you? I was sick. I knew what my mother was doing and I didn't want it to happen to Emily. My mother said is it a deal?

Ted went to his car taking Emily with him and leaving us together and for ten minutes my mother fidgeted and looked worried. I watched her but she couldn't look at me.

And then Ted, carrying a case of whiskey, came in with Emily and she was holding her white dress and she still had on her Mary Janes and she still had on her panties but she was crying. My mother said well, do we have a deal?

Ted set the case of whiskey on the floor. He pulled out his billfold and he counted four hundred bucks, fifty at a time, and handed them to my mother.

My mother pocketed the money and she said, She's all yours.

My mother shoved me ahead of her to the back of the trailer and I turned to look and Emily was standing in front of him and he had pulled down her little girl panties and I felt something horrible in me. I remembered being just like that.

When we were in the back, I told my mother I was going to take Emily and she said, Maxine, you're not going anywhere till he's through. I remember every word, Berle. Every word. And when she grabbed my arm, I took the hatchet Ted kept for cutting kindling and hit her with it.

I was too weak to kill her but she was bleeding so I hit her again and that time she fell and her coat opened and I saw that she was wearing just a pair of blue panties. She glared at me and there was pure hated in her eyes and she said, You little bitch, and so I hit her again and then Ted was behind me and he said, what the hell and he grabbed me but he stumbled on my mother's foot and I hit him in the head, hit him hard and it felt good and I was happy about it but then I looked up and Emily was there and there was a   blood stain on panties and she was in shock.

Emmy, Emmy, I said and I snatched her hand and ran out of the trailer but then I remembered her dress and so I went back in and I got her dress and I went to my mother and took the four hundred dollars she had in her pocket and I heard Ted groan and then he was quiet and so I took his billfold and all the money he had in it and then in the kitchen I turned on the gas and closed the door and outside I picked up Emily and we ran and she was crying and asking what did I do to Mommy and I told her she didn't have to worry any more Ted wasn't going to touch her and then behind me I heard the explosion and I turned to see the trailer burning and Emily said, Maxine, is Mommy dead?

I dragged her downtown. I didn't know what to do and so I took her to the Greyhound. Everyone was staring at us but I took her to the toilet and washed her off and I kissed her and tucked money into her panties then I told her I'd be right back, but I didn't go back, Berle.

I couldn't go back and I'm ashamed for that. I shouldn't have left her but we didn't have anywhere else to go and no one to help us. I had killed them and no one would help me and I remember looking at her as she stood there in her little white panties holding her dress. I never went back for her. I thought she'd be better off without me and now how do I make it up to her? How can I ever make it up to her if she won't even let me try?

Maxine stops talking then and I do the only thing I know how to do—I hold her tight and feel twenty years of guilt and shame oozing out of her and then she stops sobbing and she's asleep.

I'd seen that before—the deep sleep that comes when your bones turn to jelly and you collapse and the only thing keeping you human is your skin. I hold her until my arms go numb.

I remember the first time I saw her on the pool deck, in the sun, wearing her emerald sunglasses, her body glistening with a thin coat of sweat like an animal after a long run and I remember how she looked at me, her head tilted to one side, the cup of her bikini revealing just a hint too much of her. Exposed, she didn't adjust, but held out a hand to me as Charlie said, This is Berle, my new superintendent.

I see the ruin in her, the broken trust, the deep betrayal and I have to remember that I'm not hooked up with a normal woman her., I'm not dealing with a whole woman, a rational woman, I'm into a woman who's been stripped and abused leaving just a beautiful shell so thin a single tap will crack it open and she'll never come together again. I know that I'll have to confront Charlie. Maybe we can work out the money angle. The money.

But the head in the box. That's another hurdle.

A Walk in the Rain and the Man with Saucer Eyes

The outside air smells rainy. A veil of mist hangs on the streets rising from the hissing tires of passing cars. I like the rain at night. In the Valley, you don't walk in the rain. In the Valley no one walks and so when you hear rain, you don't want to be out there. Rain gives me a sense of mystery where there is none. Even when you think you're all worn out and there's nothing left, the rain can put some of it back. I like the feeling of being wet in the darkness, of being clean and at any minute I expect to hear myself wail, a scream that I've wanted to scream ever since I watched the Tornado taking my Dad's ketch amidships while at water level my eyes splashed with the wake and when I came up I see the Tornado split the ketch in half and then explode.

But I didn't scream then. Didn't scream when the heat of the fire made the water on my face steam, didn't scream when I smelled the gasoline fumes ripe with the odor of meat, ribs left too long on a barbecue, didn't scream when all that was left was the crackle of the fire. I just sank into the silence and into the darkness.

The hiss of tires, the mist from the pavement, mist falling around me. I remember a koan—if you walk in the mist you get wet. Maxine is the mist. I'm soaked with her, besotted with her, besotted, a strange word that worms its way out of my brain as I think of her in the room waiting for me...the first woman to wait for me. She's damaged and torn but we fit, two halves of two lives ripped apart and glued back with sex and a pile of money that doesn't belong to us. And always the message in the wooden box.

Time. My head is clear so I enter the hotel, pass the front desk where the Asian night clerk with her half shaved head and one pierced ear with its bangle six inches long looks up at me, half waves at me and if I had time I'd ask her to show me her tattoo, the one she calls a tramp stamp.

In the elevator I feel good. The walk in the rain has made everything clear and I know what I have to do.

At the door, I stop. It's half open, a sliver of light seeps into the corridor with its art deco table and art deco mirror and its art deco carpet and I hear a man's voice saying,

He needs you, Maxine.

I don't care what he needs.

He wants you back.

You mean he wants his money back.

He don't care about the money.

You get a percentage, Clyde?

You know I want you back too, Maxie.

So, no percentage, no finder's fee for catching up to the cash?

Nah. Hell, Maxine, he just wants you back.

I'm not going back.

Aw, you don't wanna be that way.

You going to carry me back in chains the way you did last time?

I can't hurt you, Maxine. You know that was just 'cause the guy was a shit.

As I listen, I wait for it to make sense. How did he know where to find her? How long has he been tracking us? What does he want? What do I do?

I push the door, see Maxine on the bed leaning against the headboard. She smokes a cigarette. Her hair like a burning bush.

Clyde stands at the foot of the bed. He wears black engineer boots, jeans, a plaid shirt. He wears a gimme cap with McGraw Concrete and Finishing stitched on it. His glasses have lenses so thick his eyes look like milk saucers. A three-day stubble. His hands are gnarly and hairy and the fingers as he reaches for the bill of his cap are thick, stubbly, dirty. Maxine says,

Berle, Clyde wants me to go back to Charlie.

I don't know what to expect. He's six four, heavy set, thick in the shoulders and thighs. His big belly gives him the heft of a tank. I look around for a weapon, see the art deco chair at the desk beside the door and as I head for it, Maxine says,

Down boys, we're just working out some details.

Clyde, the man with the thick lenses, holds up and he grins and it's a rotten tooth grin, the grin of a man who hates dentists and hasn't seen one in twenty years. His mouth, though, is kind, almost nice, the mouth of a man who, at one time must have tasted honey. I glance at Maxine. She smiles. Clyde holds out a hand.

I seen you around the plant.

Clyde's Charlie's messenger, Berle.

I heard, I say.

I squeeze the hand that squeezes back and it's not a friendly, nice squeeze but a steel-hard squeeze and he doesn't want to let go. Maxine says,

Maxine stubs out her cigarette in the art deco triangle ashtray.

What do you think I ought to do, Berle?

You'll do what you want, I say.

Now see, Maxine, Clyde says. He's got it right. You don't want no trouble, do you Berle?

I'm already in trouble.

So whacha gonna tell Charlie?

Tell Charlie we'll be up in a couple of days, Maxine says.

He won't like that, Maxine.

Fuck Charlie, Maxine says. He can eat shit for all I care.

The Woman Who Couldn't Sleep
Love Duet

For two days, we are like a couple of innocent kids. We don't have sex, we don't go out, we just hold onto each other but we're both thinking the same thing—How do we handle Charlie? How do we handle Clyde?

At three o'clock I switch on the light. Maxine is awake.

Can't go to sleep? I ask her.

I'm afraid I won't wake up.

You mean you're afraid you'll die?

I dreamed that you deserted me.

I'm not going anywhere, Maxine. I'm part of your life.

Does that mean you worry about me?

We're going back to square one and there's a head in that box and Clyde is out there waiting with his shillelagh.

So you worry about me.

If we don't go back he'll just track us down again.

Why did you stay with me?

You know why.

Say it then. Say it.

I don't want you to shut me out.

Shut you out? You've been in and out a dozen times now.

It's deeper than that. Sometimes it's like you put up a wall I can't get through and you can't see that there's this person in this room who cares about you, Maxine.

Cares about me?

All I want is for you to let me…you know…

You're blushing. Look at you. I say fuck and shit and you are a rock, but I even get close to the L word and you get embarrassed. It's really easy to say, Berle. It's not hard. L O V E.

You're right. Some things are hard for me to say so I get it done in other ways.

Say it. Stop blushing and say it. L O V E.

You make easy things hard, Maxine.

None of this equipment is worth a dime if it doesn't make you hard. Tell me, Berle, are you a leg man? A tit man? An ass man?

You don't need to talk like that. You're not a...

A what? A whore?"

That's right.

Well, I'm not Snow White unless Snow White gets paid for blow jobs.

Why do you talk like that about yourself?

You know what we're going back to, Berle. You know and you still want to get inside my head? Well, inside my head is everything I've ever been or done or said and sometimes it scares the shit out of me because it's a fucking orgy and there's a lot of blood and there are dead people and my little sister will always be in that fucking trailer whorehouse with that fucking pervert and no matter what happens it'll always be there and you've gotta ask yourself if that's what you want because that's what I am.

That's what was, Maxine. That's what was.

And that's why I can't sleep.

I know. I know. I know it's not pretty, but all I want is for it to be true.

True? Berle. In my head it's like some back-street quack keeps stirring up my brain and my insides and I'm bleeding and there's nothing anyone can do to stop it.

I cross the love divide. It's an abyss. It's a long way from L to O and there's a canyon between V and E but I do what I have to do—I hold her. Hold her tight. Feel her heat. Smell the hot metal anger. Feel the slavery in her skin

142

that's kept her in chains since the day some man took what didn't belong to him and never gave it back leaving her like this—betrayed, hurt, so beautiful in her pain that she can't understand why I'm here and what I'm doing and why I'm not leaving.

Snuggled against me, she's perfect. I wonder what she's seeing in there this time and who's with her and what is he doing to her. And in her anguish, she is perfect and soft and real and I'm not going anywhere without her. L O V E. There are times when you say things that make horror blush. Times you make terror scream. And there are times when you don't say what needs to be said and for that you rot from the inside out with the words nailed to your tongue. I should have said it. She knew I wanted to say it. But I couldn't. I just couldn't.

And then, my eyes go heavy and I drop off and it's dawn when I come back to Maxine kneeling over me and she's crying. She whispers,

Please don't make me go back.

Anatomy of a Kiss

In the half-light coming through the window, a red beacon on a tower flashes a warning I should have taken. But it's too late. She doesn't want to go, I don't want to go. I'm trapped in the room, in the hotel, in this city. Maybe forever.

She stirs, her heat roils up bringing with it the scent of hotel sheet and perfume. In the red light, her skin glistens like small red flares boiling up from inside her. Her eyes guide me to her mouth.

Her lips are soft, warm. This is why I can't get out of the room, this is why I'm helpless, chained to a block of stone.

Her hands on my neck are relentless. Her animal taste mixes with the vibrant longing as if still in half-dream, half-nightmare, she wants what she can't have. She pushes against my impatience, makes me into a toy. Her hands, as if they had a voice, ask how much I want her, how long can I wait, how much do I dare to resist? She kisses me, gentle as a bird lighting on a flower. The slight intake of anxious breath, the eruption of sweat, sweat of skin to skin. Still she plays me. Her mouth bait. Desire is a long heavy chain around my neck anchoring me to her, to this bed, to this hotel room in this city. To her. And I don't resist.

The taste in my mouth is the taste of her blooming in me, Never enough.

She mutters, leaking her own urgency, now more full blown than mine, but as if ashamed of her admission, she retreats, and now docile eyes drop from mine as she recoups her innocence, lays to rest her shame and then against the hand guiding my hand to her belly, I feel her slickness and then she pulls my hand away and raises it to my nose and I take in the flower scent of her.

She laughs, a rich laugh as if she's poking fun at my helplessness and this is why I'm still in the room, in the same bed for days, eating only what is placed at the door like a prisoner in a cell. In the laugh, there is tension as she inhales when I won't withdraw my hand, and her mouth again seeks my mouth with a shuddering intensity, and her tongue again splits my lips. I need more. I am ready. I am anxious. She feels my need in the arching of my back, belly pressed against hers, and her hands now on my hand pulling me against her and again she shudders, the ripples of her shivering like waves of a placid lake torn by a stone hurled into its calm.

She mutters, I back away to the end of the tether of her hands locked on my hips and in her eyes I see the faint flicker of red from the beacon of a tower as it reflects off the mirror on the wall and zips across her eyes. Those eyes. I feel the heat of our legs touching and then she releases my hips and gathering the hem of the sheet covering us, she lifts it, drops it, a small shaft of cool air sweeps over me and I feel a chill. She flips the sheet away and in the dim light of the street pouring through the glass, I see her stretched out against the sheet, the freckles of her skin small new black dots pocking her. I run the palms of both hands over her belly, over her chest, over her breasts, over her neck, over her face and then again the slow mating of mouth to lips and she arches against me, and I smell her new arousal, feel her arousal and this is why I am captive in the room, this is why I can't break free, this is the chain and the stone and the anchor.

If the light were stronger, I know she would be flushed from chest to cheek to forehead, the russet flush of blood urging her, an autonomic response to her arousal that says she is on the brink and any small touch, no matter how slight, will break her free and she jerks in a short breath, then another and another and the surrender in her eyes.... desire set in her jaw. I am ready, but she places a hand in the center of my chest, just where my heart hammers. I tremble with each beat. I lean against her hand. She yields, lowering me to her, but tasting her is not what I want. No. Now it is just her mouth, lips warm that intrigue me. She knows it. Like a coquette, she denies me everything while offering nothing not even promise. And I know this is, will be, the last time we will ever be this pure.

She tries to push me away but I insist, my full weight pressing against that solitary palm until she can restrain me no longer and then my mouth touches hers and her hands are no longer flowers, but knives digging into my skin, the sharp sweet arc of pain, blood just a thrust away. I kiss her, feel her rising, the rough torch of her body a fire but drenched in sweat.

This is why I am a prisoner. This is the chain. The last time. All this soon to be a memory. And then what?

She lies hair spread on the pillow in amber coils. She raises a finger to my mouth, runs the tip over my lips again tracing the entire history of where we have just been, where we are going. And she whispers, as if saying for the first time,

I love you, Berle. Please, please stay with me. Please don't leave.

Face Off

The drive up I-5 is quiet. Maxine slumps against the door smoking one Slim after another without rolling down the window. The 850 stinks but somehow, she makes smoke lose its toxicity. I remember the drive down to Portland, how she squeezed out little bits of her story until the last day in the trailer park with Emily it all came together and Maxine broke open when she realized she was alone, she couldn't save Emily, Emily didn't need her. She realized she couldn't keep running until she had some place to go and to get there she had to pass through Charlie's fire.

I glance at her curled against the door in a tight little defeated ball and I'm glad, glad to be with her, glad we're headed back to face Charlie, glad to be rid of the money that's now wrapped back in a box and sealed in the trunk of the 850 along with the shrunken head of her one-time lover and I wonder how far they got, where did they go, how did he use her? Was it ugly? Was it soft and slow? Just how?

As we top the pass at Snoqualmie, Maxine sits up and in the dash lights her face turns dark and her hair turns black and she says,

Are we there?

She lays her hand on my thigh and it is a warm hand and I'm glad she's there but I dread opening the door to Charlie's place. Still it has to be done. Maxine says,

You remember what I said last night about marriage?

Yes I do.

Maybe I was wrong.

We're all wrong more than we're right, I say.

Don't talk down to me, Berle.

I'll never talk down to you.

I can never have kids.

I know that.

Do you want kids?

It doesn't matter.

I can't see bringing a kid into this fucked up world.

It is screwed up but it doesn't have to end that way, Maxine.

How else can I get you to stay?

I'll with you, but we gotta square up with Charlie.

I hate your snotty self-righteousness.

That's the way I am, sweetheart. The detail man, remember?

You're not a detail man, you're a sanctimonious asshole.

You're stuck with me now, Maxine. I've been tested by the blackest of the black and I like where I am.

Stop it.

It's true.

What gives you the right to be Mr Clean and Pure? Nothing. You're just as fucked up as the rest of us.

Never denied it. I've got what I want. It took me a while, but I have it now.

No more whores you mean, Maxine says.

No. You're whore enough for me.

She squeezes my leg and she leans over to me and whispers in my ear that she loves it when I talk dirty to her.

Homecoming

She's silent when we approach Charlie's house on the bluff overlooking the Yakima River and I see Clyde's pick up in the drive and the lights are on in the house and a Mariachi band blares Cielo Rojo over the speakers on the pool deck and I park and shut down the 850 and Maxine says,

I'm afraid.

I open the glove box and pluck out the Taurus 9 MM and jack a cartridge into the chamber and Maxine says,

You're not going to use that are you?

Probably not.

I'd of thought you weren't a gun guy.

I'm a gun guy. You ready?

No.

Holding hands, we walk into the house, into the living room where Charlie sits in a big leather chair, his shirt off, his hairy chest black as a mat of coal, his bald head glistening with sweat, his eyes closed. Around him on the floor there are a half dozen bottles of Tecate and tucked between his thighs a half-empty quart of Cuervo tequila rests.

I shut off the stereo and the Mariachis and in the silence Charlie snorts then comes awake and he looks at me then at Maxine and he struggles to sit up and the quart of Cuervo spills onto the carpet and Charlie staggers to his feet then falls back into the chair and he says,

Took your time, dincha?

It's a long drive, I say. I tuck the Taurus in my waistband and look at Maxine who says,

Charlie, I'm sorry I took your money.

Charlie looks at me, his eyes bleary, puffy, red.. He slurs out a few words I can't catch then he clears his throat and he says in that gravel voice of his,

I don't give a shit about the money, but you, you cocksucker, you got her to fall in love with you and how in the fuck did you do that, you mother fucker?

Maxine says, Charlie, I came back to tell you to your shit-faced face that I'm leaving you and I'm leaving the money here because I don't need your fucking money. It's out the car, but I'm leaving you and I'm leaving everything else here but what I'm wearing and I don't give a shit what you think.

Charlie says, Come here, baby, come over here.

He holds out a hand and grins and tries to smile but his face won't crack and he puckers up like he's going to cry and Maxine stiffens and crosses her arms over her chest and she says,

Don't call me baby, asshole.

What can I call you? Berle's cunt? Berle's whore? You fucked me up, baby, after everything I did for you.

To me, you mean to me, you pervert.

I never did nothing you didn't want me to do, Charlie says.

What about the heads, Charlie?

Yeah, what about the heads?

I'm here because this good man made me come here but I'm not taking your crap anymore.

The granite came yesterday, Charlie says.

What?

The granite for your kitchen.

I don't give a shit about the granite.

Good cause I sent it back.

A door opens then and Clyde with the huge glasses stands at the threshold and he holds a shotgun that looks like a howitzer and Charlie says,

You remember Clyde? You gotta 'member Clyde. Did you think I was gonna just let you two run off, you cocksucker?

Don't do anything stupid, Charlie, Maxine says.

The only stupid thing I did was pull you outa the slime you were born into, you fucking cheap slut. Take'em out Clyde, both of'em.

I look at Clyde and he's looking at me and he has both hands on that shotgun so I ease the Taurus from my waistband I nod at him and he knows I'm not going to blow him away. I walk to him and lay a hand on the barrel of the gun and look him in the eyes and I say,

You don't want to do that, do you, Clyde?

Clyde, take that son of a bitch down, Charlie says.

Maxine picks up the quart of Tequila and smacks Charlie in the head and Tequila slops out but the bottle doesn't crack. Charlie crashes over the arm of the chair and he rolls onto the floor, Maxine on him, and she's screaming at him as she hits him again and I look at Clyde who shrugs and lowers the shotgun.

I break Maxine off Charlie who's bleeding from his forehead and left cheek and his eyes are black with hate and he's on his feet going after the wild Maxine but Clyde unloads the shotgun into Charlie who whirls and lunges at Clyde who jacks another shell in the shotgun and fires again and Charlie flips over onto his back, feet kicking for a second before going quiet.

Maxine is on her knees.

I'm still waiting to die.

Clyde says, Charlie never treated me right, Maxine.

Clyde, I say, you better get on the horn to 911.

You better get her outta here. I'll take care of the dickwad.

On her feet, Maxine closes on Clyde and kisses him on the cheek. She says,

You dumb bastard. You fucking dumb bastard.

You never liked any of those other guys, did you, Maxine?

No one but you, Clyde. No one but you.

You get the fuck outta here, Clyde says, I'm gonna get the chainsaw.

*****

Back in the 850, before I can crank it up, Maxine crawls over the console and straddles me and kisses me hard and I get hard, very hard and she's whispering in my ear that she loves me and wants me in her right now and she says she doesn't have any underwear on and I feel her hand unzipping me, and she giggles and she is right and she's very wet and she bites my ear and gasps and I think about clouds and butterflies and birds and the rain and the rustle of leaves but she's working her machinery hard and then with a gasp she stiffens, holds me tight in her and then collapses against me—hot and wet and steamy.

She whimpers like a cat begging for food and then she whispers in my ear,

That was fast, wasn't it, lover?

*****

She's silent as we pull into the driveway of the house I left five days ago.

It is dark and something is wrong. Maxine says,

Do we have to do this?

There're some papers. We'll need them later.

I hold the door and she enters a house that's been trashed and slashed and muck smeared over the leather sofa that's been gutted.

Maxine says, He did this.

Clyde probably.

I drag her to the bedroom and tip the bed on its side and roll the carpet up and open the floor safe and pull out the sheaf of papers—bonds, bank book, certificates that hold everything I'm worth. When I get to the stacks of hundreds and Maxine kneels and her face is flushed and she says,

Jesus Christ. All that?

You're not the only one who took Charlie for a ride, I say.

What? What if he'd found this?

He didn't but that's why we're back here.

You don't get upset about anything do you?

It's just things, Maxine.

You had all that cash and you played games with me? Asshole.

I kiss her and she's hot and tight against me and she whispers that she fucked up my whole life and I say,

It's doesn't matter when you're starting over.

You really want to do that?

I'm doing it, I say. Come on. We have to get.

What about the house? You gonna just leave the house?

After dropping the papers in the 850, I lead Maxine back to the garage where I have two five-gallon jerrycans of gas. Maxine says oh and follows me back inside.

A House on Fire

I pour the gasoline on the sofa, slosh it out across the carpet, soak the beds, and dump towels on the bathroom floors and load them up. The smell of gas is strong.

Maxine, standing by the front door says,

Are you sure you want to do this?

Can't not do it, I say.

Say some kids dumped it looking for dope.

We're in it all the way, Maxine. You burned up your past, I'll burn up mine.

This isn't maybe the best way to end it.

You better go outside now, I say.

I go when you go.

Then you get to light the fire.

I look at her. She shrugs. I pull the book of matches from my shirt pocket. Hand it to her.
Standing beside her at the threshold I look over the destroyed living room, the sofa gutted, the easy chairs slashed, paneling ripped from the walls, light fixtures pulled from the ceiling where wires dangle down like bloody stalactites dripping from the roof of a cave.

Just things, I say to her, just things. But for a second I don't want to do it, don't want to turn it to ash, but I have to end it if I want to start over. I have to let go of everything that means anything to me and the house is the last connection to the my parents, the last part of my old life still standing. I say,

Go ahead.

She strikes the first match and flicks it into the living room. The air explodes, heat rushing at us in sudden waves. I remember floating in Lake Wallula watching my dad's ketch explode as the Tornado tore her guts out. I remember the heat of that fire as she burned down to the waterline.

We back away from the crackling flames. Maxine circles her arms around my waist. She squeezes me tight. I say,

What do you think?

Now we're even more alike, she says.

Is this how it looked? The trailer?

This is a half million-dollar house. The trailer was a whorehouse on wheels.

Both burn the same way, I say. What did the cops say?

You read it in the clippings, Maxine says. Fire of unknown origin claims two.

Do you regret it?

I never regret.

The fire heats up, windows explode, a rain of glass, flames shoot through the frames, smoke roils up against the nighttime sky and in the red and yellow flames. Fire breaks through the ceiling. I feel a release as if something has just sprung loose—but at the same time there's the sense that I've lost something I'll never have again. Maxine whispers,

Won't be long till someone reports it. We better go.

*****

I open the door of the 850. Maxine slides in. Without looking back, I start the car and head for 82.

Maxine sits, knees tucked under her. She says,

Thank you.

For?

For doing this for me. I can never thank you.

You already have, I say, and you'll pay a lot of interest from here on.

She laughs. Behind me, in the mirror, I see the rosy aura of the burning house. Everything I have is now in the car—a few clothes, the papers, the cash, the pistol. The essentials. And in the trunk there is a box holding a shrunken head and beside it a box jammed with four hundred and fifty thousand dollars in it. Good money. No strings now, no dirt now, now just hard cash that will buy anything anyplace anytime.

Maxine rummages in her sack purse and pulls out a pack of Slims. I reach for her hand and press the pack of cigarettes tight. She looks at me. I say,

Can you quit?

She lifts my hand from the pack of Slims and drops it in her lap. Then she rolls down the window. The wind bites hot and dry in the car and in the air, I smell the lingering remains of gasoline on my skin, the odor of burnt wood, the acrid nip of scorched hair. Maxine tosses the cigarettes out the window and then, digging in the purse again, she plucks out the gold lighter and drops it out the window. She lets the window blow into the car flipping her hair in the turbulence. She says,

How different will we be?

Where do you want to go? I say.

I don't know. Somewhere there aren't any republicans.

San Francisco?

I've never been to San Francisco.

They call it The City, I say. It's a good place to live. It's kind of like another country where they speak English. I know a place, Sausalito—water everywhere, hills. Fog. Chinese food. I got a little shack there.

I love Chinese food, Maxine says. I don't know how long it's been since I had good Chinese food. A shack?

We'll eat good Chinese, I say. Chinatown is huge now. It's not just North Beach. Yeah, just a little three-room shack.

I don't know where North Beach is.

Imagine five square miles of Chinese restaurants and trinkets made in Hong Kong. Everything you could ever want.

Maxine leans against my shoulder. It feels good to have her touch me. She says,

We really should have had Clyde burn Charlie's money.

A dead man doesn't need cash, I say.

I mean, that way, I'd feel better.

Clyde took care of it as far as I'm concerned, I say. He'll burn the heads and the boxes.

Will they be looking for us?

Probably. Maybe. I don't know.

What will we do?

We'll manage, I say. You can lose yourself in the City. It's big enough you can feel good about not knowing your neighbors.

So it's San Francisco, she says.

If you don't want republicans.

I like you Berle.

Like me? We're way beyond like, don't you think?

You know what I mean.

So now you're the one having trouble with the L word.

What L word is that?

L O V E.

Oh, that word.

She leans into me and bites my ear and slides her hand across my thigh. She says, So you can spell it, Mr. Kubiak.

MAXINE

Jack Remick

Jack Remick is a novelist and a poet. His work has appeared around the country.

Coffeetown Press published *The California Quartet—The Deification, Valley Boy, The Book of Changes,* and *Trio of Lost Souls.*

Gabriela and The Widow was a finalist for the Montaigne Award.

Blood, a companion novel to *No Century for Apologies* and *Doubles in a Game of Chance,* was published by Camel Press, an imprint of Coffeetown.

Remick is co-author, with Robert J. Ray, of *The Weekend Novelist Writes a Mystery.*

Remick's poetry includes *Josie Delgado, a poem of the Central Valley, Satori—Poems,* and work in *The Seattle Five Plus One.*

He has other work in various anthologies including *Raven Chronicles V/ 26, The Helicon West Anthology,* and *So Much Depends Upon,* (a Red Wheelbarrow Writers Anthology).